ORCA
Think

Question, connect and take action to become better citizens
with a brighter future. Now that's smart thinking!

ALL CONSUMING

SHOP SMARTER FOR THE PLANET

ERIN SILVER

ILLUSTRATED BY
SUHARU OGAWA

ORCA BOOK PUBLISHERS

Published in Canada and the United States in 2024 by Orca Book Publishers.
orcabook.com

Library and Archives Canada Cataloguing in Publication
Title: All consuming : shop smarter for the planet / Erin Silver ; illustrated by Suharu Ogawa.
Names: Silver, Erin, 1980- author. | Ogawa, Suharu, 1979- illustrator.
Series: Orca think ; 16.
Description: Series statement: Orca think ; 16 | Includes bibliographical references and index.
Identifiers: Canadiana (print) 20230563074 | Canadiana (ebook) 20230563082 |
ISBN 9781459835979 (hardcover) | ISBN 9781459835986 (PDF) | ISBN 9781459835993 (EPUB)
Subjects: LCSH: Consumption (Economics)—Environmental aspects—Juvenile literature. | LCSH: Commercial products—Environmental aspects—Juvenile literature. | LCSH: Consumer behavior—Environmental aspects—Juvenile literature. | LCSH: Shopping—Environmental aspects—Juvenile literature. | LCSH: Young consumers—Juvenile literature. | LCSH: Social action—Juvenile literature. | LCGFT: Instructional and educational works.
Classification: LCC HC79.C6 S55 2024 | DDC j339.4/7—dc23

Library of Congress Control Number: 2023948859

Summary: Part of the nonfiction Orca Think series for middle-grade readers, this illustrated book examines disposable culture, its effect on the planet and practical ways young people can use their purchasing power.

Orca Book Publishers is committed to reducing the consumption of nonrenewable resources in the production of our books. We make every effort to use materials that support a sustainable future.

Orca Book Publishers gratefully acknowledges the support for its publishing programs provided by the following agencies: the Government of Canada, the Canada Council for the Arts and the Province of British Columbia through the BC Arts Council and the Book Publishing Tax Credit.

Cover and interior artwork by Suharu Ogawa
Design by Troy Cunningham
Edited by Kirstie Hudson

Printed and bound in South Korea.

27   26   25   24   •   1   2   3   4

*To Kesh, whose love, creativity and potential
to effect positive change are limitless.*

ALL CONSUMING
SHOP SMARTER FOR THE PLANET

CONTENTS

INTRODUCTION

Like many kids, you probably think a lot about buying things—everything from the latest-model phone to the coolest outfits, fast food to gift cards for friends' birthdays. These days you can buy just about anything online and have it delivered before you even finish your homework. And when it breaks or you don't need it anymore, you can just throw it away. In many places around the world, culture has become disposable—we see something we want, we buy it, and then we throw it away to make room for something new. Most of the time these decisions are made faster than the time it takes to send a text message.

You might be surprised to learn that all those things people like to buy—clothes, food, gifts and technology— are not great for the planet. You might feel like you're too

Have you ever thought about how your purchases impact the planet?

young to help, but that's not true. In fact, there's actually a big thing you can do, starting today. You can use your shopping habits to send a message to companies around the world. It's called "putting your money where your mouth is," and it makes adults in powerful positions listen up.

Need proof? In 1989, when I was still ordering Happy Meals, children across the United States boycotted McDonald's and wrote letters to the restaurant's headquarters demanding that the chain stop selling food in Styrofoam boxes. Some even mailed greasy containers to local stores to protest the clamshell packaging that's bad for the planet. When the media caught on, McDonald's was forced to act. Today the restaurant chain uses recycled paper, wooden cutlery and paper straws—it has done a good job cutting back on waste. In Canada alone, McDonald's has cut its plastic waste by 840 tons (762 metric tons) a year. In the United States, its changes have reduced waste by 30 percent over the last several years.

Even young kids can make a difference. Sorting and properly recycling plastics is just one of many ways to help.
ARTMARIE/GETTY IMAGES

A global survey of 10,000 youth found that 95 percent are worried about *climate change*, and 60 percent are "extremely" or "very" worried. Worse, 57 percent reported that climate change made them feel "powerless." This book will show you how you can help. You can use your purchasing power to effect positive change. This book isn't going to tell you to stop shopping, but it will show you that what you buy matters. By making even small changes to what you put in your cart, you can make a huge impact on the environment one purchase at a time.

2

CHAPTER ONE

Cheap and Chic T-shirts

Have you ever heard of *retail therapy*? It's the rush of joy you get from buying something new, especially on a day that hasn't gone your way. Those happy feelings soar when your friends compliment you on your cool new sneakers or your shirt. Unfortunately, the great feeling we get from shopping tends to last about three wears, or maybe even one month, before those new items seem old. Then we cast them aside and go back to the mall or shop online for more. Much more.

CUPBOARDS FULL OF CLOTHES

A charity called TRAID found that in London, 23 percent of clothes in people's closets aren't even worn. In other

Does your closet look like this? Often clothes are made and sold cheaply, so we buy more than we need—and we don't think twice about throwing items away when we don't want to wear them anymore.
LIUDMILA CHERNETSKA/GETTY IMAGES

An estimated 85 percent of the clothes bought by Americans end up in the garbage. That amounts to about 80 pounds (36 kilograms) of clothes per person per year, or the weight of a Bernese mountain dog!

wealthy countries, the average person buys 60 percent more clothes than they did 15 years ago, but now those clothes are kept for half as long. By the time you're graduating from high school (or around 2030), people could be buying 63 percent more—that equals more than 500 billion extra T-shirts. Imagine trying to stuff all those shirts into a drawer!

It all adds up to an extra-large problem for the environment. Our shopping habits impact the planet and even the workers who make our clothes. But retail therapy doesn't have to be bad for the planet. With a few simple changes, shopping can become more **sustainable**.

SEW IT BEGINS

You probably don't know how to sew—at least, not well enough to make your own shirts, pants and dresses or even mend a hole in your sock. A long time ago, before there were factories and stores and malls, people made everything themselves, from their bread to their furniture to their clothes. Then, in 1769, Scottish inventor James Watt changed everything when he patented his steam engine. Others quickly realized that

this engine technology could power machines to make and sew cloth, among other things. Factories were built across Europe and then North America. Families flocked to cities to work in factories. Even children worked there. People became too busy to make things themselves, so they started buying manufactured products, including clothes.

With the invention of the steam engine, factories could produce large amounts of clothing very quickly. Until child labor laws were put in place, many factory employees were children.

CLOTHING CHANGES

Then came the roaring twenties—a time between World War I and World War II when people had money to spend. Factory owners realized they could sell more if they had new products to offer. They started making clothes in new colors and styles. Even new models of cars rolled off the assembly lines. Advertisers got smart too. They created ads for radio and newspapers that convinced people they needed to buy the latest and greatest. People bought things they wanted, even if they didn't need them. That meant they purchased new things before the old things had worn out. The Great Depression and World War II made being *frugal* a way to help the war effort on the home front. People darned their socks or made do with what they had because they didn't have a choice—and it was their duty. But after the war, people went back to work and the money flowed again. They bought fridges, televisions, houses with double-car garages and, of course, clothes. Scientists and environmentalists began to realize that all these factories, making all these goods, were polluting the planet. But things were about to get worse...

FASHION DISASTER

By the 1960s and '70s, young people took fashion in another direction. They wanted trendy, cheaply made clothing so they could express themselves through what they wore—and manufacturers wanted to deliver. By the 2000s, people in wealthy countries were addicted to *fast fashion*—inexpensive, cheaply made, trendy clothes that were only meant to last a short while before they were thrown away. Today some of our

clothes are cheaper than a smoothie, and they're just as disposable as the cup.

Global shopping habits have led fashion brands to open manufacturing plants, also called **sweatshops**, in **developing countries** where they can get people to work longer hours in poor conditions at a fraction of what they would be paid in developed countries. It means companies like H&M, Topshop, Zara and Forever 21 can churn out clothes faster and cheaper than ever before. For example, Zara produces an estimated 840 million garments a year and can launch styles within about two weeks from the time they're seen on the runway or at an awards show. And clothing companies like this don't have to worry about labor or environmental laws getting in their way. That's because the countries where fast fashion is made—countries like Bangladesh, Vietnam, China and the Philippines—don't have strict laws to break. Today, both people and the planet are mistreated, all for the sake of fashion.

FASHION VICTIM ONE: WORKERS

Clothing and footwear production is a $2.4 trillion industry, but who makes our track pants and sneakers? Around the world, more than 60 million people work to make our clothes and shoes. Some of those are children. UNICEF estimates that more than 100 million children are affected by the industry—as workers, as children of working parents and by conditions in the communities in which garment workers live. These workers live in some of the world's poorest countries. They work in buildings without proper air quality. They don't get days off or go home to play video games and ride bikes. Many work 14 to 16 hours a day, seven

A lot of our clothes are made in countries like Vietnam, where workers aren't paid enough to live comfortably.

PAUL PRESCOTT/DREAMSTIME.COM

days a week. And when they make clothes, they're exposed to dangerous chemicals.

You'd think these workers would be making lots of money with all that overtime. But that's not true. Half of garment workers aren't even paid enough to live comfortably. In Vietnam, the second-largest supplier of America's clothes and shoes after China, only 1 percent of workers earn a *living wage*—the minimum amount people need to earn to afford basic needs. In developed countries, many people belong to unions or are protected by employment laws, which help people get better working conditions and fair pay. Yet the majority of people who make our clothes—90 percent—don't have these kinds of rights.

HOLDING SWEATSHOPS ACCOUNTABLE

The issue caught the world's attention when tragedy struck on April 24, 2013. On that day garment workers—mostly women and children—were crushed when the eight-story Rana Plaza building in Bangladesh collapsed. It was the deadliest garment-factory disaster in history, killing 1,134 workers and injuring another 2,500. The world watched in horror. How could billion-dollar brands allow this to happen?

Designers and changemakers got together and created a way for shoppers to demand that the fashion industry be more accountable. In 2014 they created a hashtag for social media called #WhoMadeMyClothes. They wanted to push companies to do a better job of paying workers fairly and making sure working conditions were safe. They also wanted companies to be open about their impact on the environment. It became the number one hashtag on Twitter that year,

and it also encouraged garment workers to launch their own hashtag—#IMadeYourClothes—to add to the conversation.

Change and transparency are still needed. Many major fashion brands are still using sweatshops to make their clothing. They are underpaying their workers and making people work long hours in unsafe factories—and they're doing it illegally. Governments, activists and advocates have stepped in to help. While the **United Nations** is targeting businesses, others are targeting consumers—people like us. You can show your support for brands that take care of people and the planet by purchasing them whenever you can.

Workers were killed when the Rana Plaza building collapsed in 2013. When buying clothes, it's important to think about whether they were made by companies that treat their workers properly.
BAYAZID AKTER/DREAMSTIME.COM

FASHION VICTIM TWO: THE ENVIRONMENT

The clothing industry creates about 1.3 billion tons (1.2 billion metric tons) of **greenhouse gas** emissions every year—more than some international airlines. If global shopping habits

continue to grow, clothes could be responsible for generating 26 percent of carbon emissions by 2050, instead of about 10 percent today. These figures don't even include the environmental damage caused when clothes are dyed, made, shipped, delivered, bought, washed or thrown away. To understand how people's clothing choices are hurting the planet, it's important to start from the ground up.

WATER

T-shirts, jeans and many other products we use every day are often made from cotton. The fabric is breathable and **biodegrades**. But growing cotton requires a lot of water. In fact, it takes about 713 gallons (2,700 liters) of water to grow enough cotton to make one T-shirt. That's enough drinking water to last one person two and a half years. It takes about 2,000 gallons (7,500 liters) of water to make a pair of jeans—the same as what one person drinks over seven years.

Eleven percent of the world's **pesticides** and 24 percent of all insecticides are used in the production of nonorganic cotton. These chemicals spread through the air, into the water and through the soil, harming plants, animals and marine life. The poison also causes higher rates of tuberculosis, stroke and cancer. So much water has been used to water cotton fields that the Aral Sea—once a large saltwater lake the size of Ireland—had almost completely dried up by 2014. It only took about 50 years for this landscape to change completely.

POLLUTION

The chemicals used to produce, dye, bleach and wash fabric can cause so much pollution that some water bodies are now toxic.

The Citarum River in Indonesia and the Pearl River in China are both contaminated by factories. They dump leftover water from the dyeing process into ditches, streams and rivers. India's Cooum River is ranked as the most polluted. Once drinkable, the water is now described as a toxic stew. Industrial waste and human sewage have created conditions that can cause cancer and other health problems.

The problem is huge—because of the dyeing and treatment process the fashion industry is the second-largest water polluter in the world, causing 20 percent of all industrial water pollution worldwide.

Many rivers like this one are polluted because of the way clothing factories dump dyes and chemicals into the water. This pollution affects the people living in those areas, who need that water to survive.
BASTIAN AS/SHUTTERSTOCK.COM

PRICE CHECK

What about those shopping bags? Every year we use billions of plastic shopping bags. They aren't recycled and end up in landfills and oceans. Governments around the world have started to ban plastic bags, but you can take action yourself by switching to reusable cloth or paper bags.

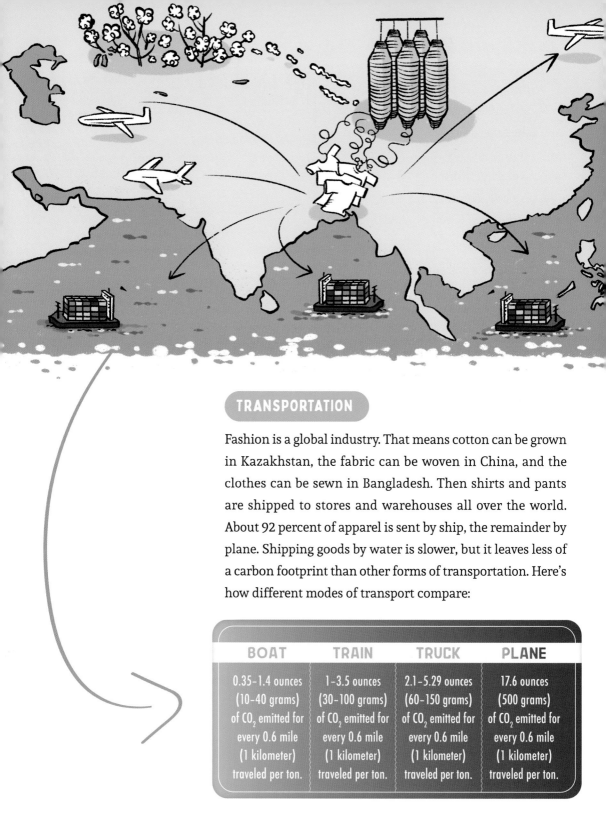

TRANSPORTATION

Fashion is a global industry. That means cotton can be grown in Kazakhstan, the fabric can be woven in China, and the clothes can be sewn in Bangladesh. Then shirts and pants are shipped to stores and warehouses all over the world. About 92 percent of apparel is sent by ship, the remainder by plane. Shipping goods by water is slower, but it leaves less of a carbon footprint than other forms of transportation. Here's how different modes of transport compare:

BOAT	TRAIN	TRUCK	PLANE
0.35–1.4 ounces (10–40 grams) of CO_2 emitted for every 0.6 mile (1 kilometer) traveled per ton.	1–3.5 ounces (30–100 grams) of CO_2 emitted for every 0.6 mile (1 kilometer) traveled per ton.	2.1–5.29 ounces (60–150 grams) of CO_2 emitted for every 0.6 mile (1 kilometer) traveled per ton.	17.6 ounces (500 grams) of CO_2 emitted for every 0.6 mile (1 kilometer) traveled per ton.

While you can't control how goods travel around the globe, you can decide how you shop—and who you buy from. Clothing that's made in North America will travel shorter distances and is most likely to travel by truck. And if you buy it locally, especially if you can walk to the store, you support businesses in your own community. But people don't tend to shop local because clothing made in faraway places is less expensive to produce.

You can also make more of your purchases online, which can actually be better for the planet than driving from store to store—unless you get two-day free shipping. Here's why fast free shipping is a problem. Say you order new underwear, a T-shirt and a phone case. If only the T-shirt is in stock at the warehouse, it will be shipped first. Everything else will be delivered in a separate box and delivered by another truck. That means more trucks are on the road, contributing emissions to the atmosphere. However, delivery services like the United States Postal Service (USPS) are trying to fix this problem. They're finding more efficient routes and using emission-free vehicles to make online shopping greener.

PRICE CHECK

Online shopping is so easy that one in five people even shop from the bathroom! In 2021 the United States Postal Service (USPS) delivered 7.6 billion packages—up from 5.7 billion just five years earlier. During the holidays, USPS delivers more than 850 million packages.

WASHING

Over 30 billion loads of laundry are done in North America each year. Each load can release 700,000 or more microfibers, or **microplastics**, into the wastewater system. Microplastics are tiny particles of plastic less than 0.2 inches (5 centimeters) in diameter—about the size of a sesame seed. They are found in synthetic clothing and even products like toothpaste. They are so small that they can pass through wastewater treatment

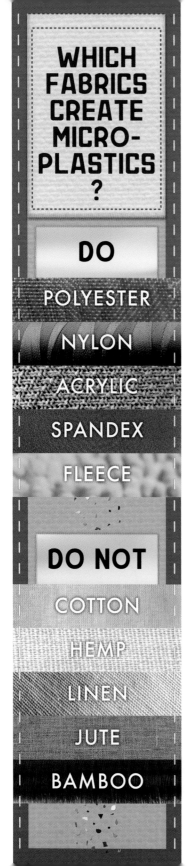

WHICH FABRICS CREATE MICRO-PLASTICS?

DO

POLYESTER

NYLON

ACRYLIC

SPANDEX

FLEECE

DO NOT

COTTON

HEMP

LINEN

JUTE

BAMBOO

plants and enter our waterways and oceans, where they threaten aquatic organisms and their habitats. Drying clothes isn't any better for the planet. One study by the City University of Hong Kong found that tumble dryers are a big cause of microfiber pollution. A single dryer can release 120 million airborne microfibers every year. When inhaled they can have adverse effects on our health and even damage organs. Washers and dryers aren't the only problems. North Americans do so many loads of laundry that 700 million plastic detergent jugs are dumped into landfills across the continent every year.

DISPOSING

People around the world collectively buy over 80 billion new items a year—four times what your parents did 20 years ago. But we keep our clothes for half as long. Put another way, today we throw away half of our cheap clothes less than a year after we buy them. Globally, people throw away enough clothes to fill one garbage truck every second, stuff the Empire State Building in four and a half hours or fill the Sydney Harbour every year.

Even worse than sending clothes to the landfill is *incinerating* them. Burning trash, including clothes, releases greenhouse gases into the air at a rate of 2,988 pounds (1,355 kilograms) of *carbon dioxide (CO$_2$)* per megawatt-hour—more than burning coal and natural gas. Governments are trying to help. The UK government wants to ban burning clothes that can be reused or recycled.

TAKING ACTION

It's possible to love fashion and still take action. It means moving from a *linear* versus *circular* way of thinking. In other words, instead of the typical "buy-use-dispose" system, we can find more ways to reuse or repurpose our clothes into something new for ourselves or for somebody else. Here are just a few of the many exciting "wardrobe changes" unfolding in the fashion community today.

Adidas has teamed up with Parley for the Oceans, a nonprofit organization that's tackling the plastic in the oceans. They've collaborated on a range of sneakers—adidas x Parley—made of a polyester yarn spun from recycled ocean waste, plastic bottles and illegal deep-sea gill nets. Adidas also conducts life-cycle assessments to understand how their products impact the planet.

The French company Veja uses only ecological materials in its shoes. Rubber for soles is sourced sustainably from rubber tappers (people who collect latex from rubber trees without harming the trees) in the Amazon rainforest. Water-repellent mesh is made from recycled plastic bottles collected on the streets of Rio de Janeiro and São Paulo. Every pair of sneakers takes three plastic bottles out of the garbage stream.

A London-based brand named Charlie Feist reclaims and recycles plastic bottles and uses them to make backpacks, bags and wallets. Most of the items they make are black. Why? Black matches everything, it's a bestseller and the color will always be in style. If you think of cost-per-wear (the cost of the item divided by the number of times you wear it), black can be worn more often than, say, lime green, giving you more "bag for your buck."

PRICE CHECK

I was watching the news one night when a story grabbed my attention. A children's clothing store called Carter's was caught cutting up unsold clothes and throwing them in the trash. These clothes could have been used by people in need, but instead they were ruined. Other stores commit this fashion crime too. In 2017 Nike was found guilty of ruining unworn sneakers and clothes. Between 2013 and 2017, H&M was accused of incinerating unsold clothing worth $4.3 billion, and in 2018 luxury brand Burberry burned more than $33 million in clothes, accessories and perfume. It's a cheap way for brands—especially luxury brands—to stop their products from being stolen or sold for less. It's how they ensure that their products are "exclusive." But when the public found out, people were upset. Burberry stopped burning clothes right away. The Environmental Protection Agency believes over 3 million tons (2.7 million metric tons) of clothes are incinerated each year.

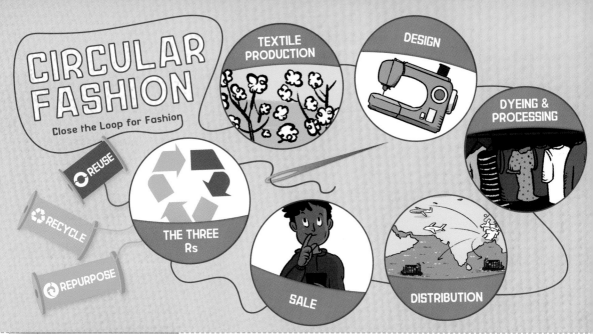

CIRCULAR FASHION

Close the Loop for Fashion

REUSE
RECYCLE
REPURPOSE

THE THREE Rs

TEXTILE PRODUCTION

DESIGN

DYEING & PROCESSING

SALE

DISTRIBUTION

LIKE

REUSE

Students at Tecumseh Public School in Halton, Ontario, were shocked to learn how much our clothes impact the planet. They made posters and organized a clothing drive. One poster read

Hello! I am a grey cardigan. I am from China (the other side of the world). And if you throw me out, I will go to the landfill... so please pass me on!

When the clothing collection was over, students had contributed 1,168 pounds (530 kilograms) of clothing, all of which could be reused.

Tentree, a clothing company based in Regina, Saskatchewan, plants 10 trees for every garment it produces. Its goal is to plant one billion trees in communities around the world by 2030. Not only do trees absorb CO_2 from the air, but they also restore habitat for wildlife. Tentree makes clothes in a way that leaves the smallest possible footprint. Its sweatshirts, for example, are made using 75 percent less water than any other hoodie in your closet. The company also creates circular supply chains by reusing leftover materials to make other products.

According to some estimates, 8 to 10 million plastic and wire hangers are made and sold every year. Only 15 percent are ever recycled. A French designer named Roland Mouret teamed up with a company in Amsterdam to establish Blue, a hanger made with 80 percent plastic waste plucked from rivers. Even though it's called Blue, the hangers are actually gray, which means no chemicals were used to make them. Just like Tentree's products, the Blue hanger has a circular lifespan—it can be recycled over and over.

18

COURTESY OF SOPHIA YANG

THREADING CHANGE

Many nonprofits, fashion brands and non-governmental organizations are working to change the way our clothes are made and the impact they have on people and the planet. Threading Change was founded by Sophia Yang in May 2020. After realizing there weren't many young or South Asian people talking about the impact of fast fashion at the UN Climate Negotiations, Sophia took action. She established an organization led by young people that's devoted to changing fashion for the better.

In 2022 she received the City of Vancouver's Greenest City Leadership award. "Winning this award feels so surreal," Yang said on social media. "This award is dedicated to all of the garment workers and heroes from across the world. The ones who are up night and day, the ones that have found ways to engage the industry despite how corrupt and unjust it is, the ones who deserve better, and inspire me endlessly to do the work that I do at Threading Change."

In 2021 Sophia was on the Corporate Knights' 30 Under 30 list of sustainability leaders. In an article about her work, Yang talked about how much she has to accomplish and how she will continue to talk to people—from kids to the elderly—about ethical fashion and human rights. Inspired by environmental activist David Suzuki when she was 12 years old, Yang continues to work hard to realize her mission to achieve the 6Fs—a feminist, fossil-fuel-free fashion future.

Tru Earth, a company in British Columbia, is helping the planet one load of laundry at a time. Instead of selling detergent in a pod or gigantic plastic jug, the founders invented an eco-friendly solution—the eco-strip. It's a dry strip of detergent that fits in a recyclable envelope. The package of strips weighs 94 percent less than a jug of traditional detergent. If everyone switched to using eco-strips, it would eliminate the need for one billion plastic jugs.

FASHION FORWARD

So what does the future of fashion look like? Expect a lot of growth, especially since new fabrics are being made from plants.

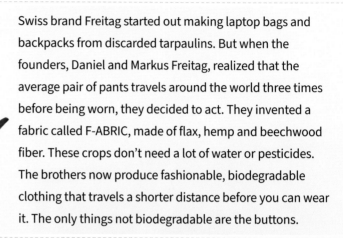

Swiss brand Freitag started out making laptop bags and backpacks from discarded tarpaulins. But when the founders, Daniel and Markus Freitag, realized that the average pair of pants travels around the world three times before being worn, they decided to act. They invented a fabric called F-ABRIC, made of flax, hemp and beechwood fiber. These crops don't need a lot of water or pesticides. The brothers now produce fashionable, biodegradable clothing that travels a shorter distance before you can wear it. The only things not biodegradable are the buttons.

You might not like the taste of mushrooms, but scientists at MycoWorks, a company in San Francisco, are finding ways to turn these fungi into leather-look jackets. Made from the rootlike structure in mushrooms called *mycelium*, the material is strong, flexible, breathable and durable. A whole cowhide of "leather" can be grown in two months. Mushrooms can be grown without a lot of space or energy, and you can compost them. You can even change the look and texture of the fabric and grow it around zippers and buttons on pants and jackets.

Piñatex is a new material made from the leaf fiber of a pineapple plant. A company called Tooche in Latvia makes shoes and bags using wool felt and Piñatex. The fabric is soft, light, warm and sustainable. Tooche always packs its products in reusable cotton bags and boxes made of recycled cardboard. Workers are paid fairly, and there is zero tolerance for discrimination.

An Italian company called Orange Fiber has found a way to make a silklike fabric from orange peels. The company works out of a juice-processing plant in Sicily, where it gets 700,000 tons (635,029 metric tons) of citrus fruit waste a year for free. The company turns the cellulose from orange rinds into yarn that can be dyed and combined with other fabrics to make high-end, sustainable fabric.

Bananatex is a waterproof fabric made from abacá fiber. The abacá plant is a relative of the banana and is grown in the Philippines. It can be planted with other crops, preventing soil erosion and helping restore the local ecosystem by giving threatened species a new home.

HOW TO SHOP SUSTAINABLY

You might not be able yet to fill your closet with clothes made from vegetables, but there *are* other things you can do to shop sustainably, starting now. And they don't involve wearing scratchy fabrics in earth tones, spending a ton of money on sustainable brands or looking for tags that say clothes are environmentally friendly. Here are some ways to do that.

Wear and share clothes you already own. If you need an outfit for a special occasion, borrow from your sibling. Lend an outfit to a friend. Try wearing clothes in different ways—roll up the legs of your jeans for a new look or bunch up your oversized T-shirt and tie it at the side.

Go thrifting. You can find tons of great vintage items by shopping at thrift or consignment stores. These are places where people drop off used items they no longer want so others can discover them.

Prom dresses are the perfect kind of item to buy secondhand, since most people wear them only once. You'll likely find something suits your style in a thrift store.
ARTMARIE/GETTY IMAGES

LIKE

REDUCE

Student journalists Seohee Hong and Elaine Hans were first-place winners in their age group in the 2021 Young Reporters for the Environment Canadian National Competition. They wrote an article about how reusable face masks are better for the planet than disposable. They reported that in 2020 "more than 1.5 billion masks were dumped into oceans...Being made primarily of plastic, they will take centuries to decompose." They also showed that the weight of medical waste being produced each day equaled the weight of three space shuttles.

Mend clothing. Sign up for a sewing class and learn how to make your own fashions or become an expert with a needle and thread. Or take your pants to get hemmed by a local tailor. I took my favorite pair of boots to a shoe-repair expert for new soles. Now they're good as new!

You can rent a tuxedo for prom and even a graduation dress from sites like Girl Meets Dress, Rent the Runway, Front Row and Wear the Walk. You choose something in your style and size, then return it when you're done. You can even rent graduation gowns and hats for your entire class.

Wash smarter. If your towel and jeans aren't dirty, don't wash them. When you do a wash, make sure the machine is full and use cold water instead of hot. Use a washing bag from a company such as Stop! MicroWaste to prevent microplastics from getting into the sewer system. Check out the detergent you use—some are better for the planet than others. Hang your clothes to dry to save energy and stop microplastics from entering the air.

PRICE CHECK

Sixty-three percent of our clothes are made from environmentally unfriendly fabrics like nylon, rayon, viscose and polyester. These fabrics are made from petrochemicals (chemicals derived from natural gas or petroleum) and contain plastic, materials that are bad for people and the planet.

Shopping at thrift stores is a great way to get cool new clothes and save them from the landfill.
JOOS MIND/GETTY IMAGES

Upcycle. Your favorite pair of jeans are now too short. Don't throw them out. Instead cut them into jean shorts. You can even turn jeans into bags, and sweatshirt sleeves into scrunchies. Go online for how-to videos or get your hands on a crafting book.

Buy sustainable brands and items. Some companies go the extra mile for the planet. Look for tags that say **Certified B Corporation**, which means the garment was made with recyclable materials. The **Global Organic Textile Standard (GOTS)** stamp means the product has at least 70 percent organic natural fibers and no toxic dyes and that workers were treated properly. When clothes are **Cradle to Cradle Certified**, it means products are safe, have a circular lifespan and responsibly made.

Donate. Go through your closet even once a year and set aside items you don't wear. If they're in good condition, donate them to friends, relatives or charities. Donating keeps these items from ending up in a landfill.

Buy less. Before you buy something, think about what's already in your closet. Do you really need this item, or do you just want it? If you're shopping online, leave the item in your cart and think about it.

PUTTING THEIR BEST FOOT FORWARD

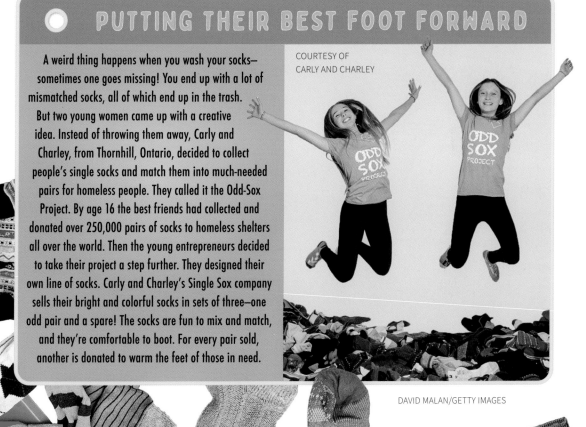

A weird thing happens when you wash your socks—sometimes one goes missing! You end up with a lot of mismatched socks, all of which end up in the trash. But two young women came up with a creative idea. Instead of throwing them away, Carly and Charley, from Thornhill, Ontario, decided to collect people's single socks and match them into much-needed pairs for homeless people. They called it the Odd-Sox Project. By age 16 the best friends had collected and donated over 250,000 pairs of socks to homeless shelters all over the world. Then the young entrepreneurs decided to take their project a step further. They designed their own line of socks. Carly and Charley's Single Sox company sells their bright and colorful socks in sets of three—one odd pair and a spare! The socks are fun to mix and match, and they're comfortable to boot. For every pair sold, another is donated to warm the feet of those in need.

COURTESY OF
CARLY AND CHARLEY

DAVID MALAN/GETTY IMAGES

CHAPTER TWO

Would You Like Fries with That?

People love fast food—burgers, fries, pizza, chicken fingers and even soda. One study found that 34 percent of Americans aged 2 to 19 eat fast food every day. That means if there are 30 students in your class, about 10 will head off for a hamburger after school—if they didn't already have cafeteria fries for lunch. Meanwhile the food-delivery business exploded when the COVID-19 pandemic started in 2020. From Australia to the United States, the demand for food delivery is now four to seven times bigger than it was in 2018.

We know that cooking at home is better for our health and that having too much greasy, fried, salty and sugary food isn't good for our bodies. But it turns out that fast food is also unhealthy for the planet. We'll look at some reasons why and dig into the ways the food industry is cooking up more sustainable solutions.

It's easier than ever to order food online, but all that fast food comes in containers. Some companies are finding sustainable solutions.
OSCAR WONG/GETTY IMAGES

TRASH TALK

I recently ordered takeout from my favorite Japanese restaurant. When my family was done eating, I felt sick. Not because of the food—my teriyaki was delicious—but because it came packed in Styrofoam containers to keep the food hot and prevent leakage. Styrofoam is the most common kind of fast-food garbage. It takes 500 years or more for it to break down in a landfill. While it's there, Styrofoam pollutes our groundwater and releases toxins into the air.

It's not just my meal that's contributing to the problem—it's the fast food, takeout and delivery meals all over the world. Some experts say half a pound of food is wasted per meal in restaurants, adding up to billions of pounds of food every year. Add to that all the wrappers, straws, boxes, bags,

I was shocked and embarrassed when I realized how much Styrofoam waste was created by a single takeout order.
ERIN SILVER

cutlery and tiny packets of ketchup you got with your last order. It's no wonder that fast-food packaging contributes almost half of the garbage found on American streets.

But there are more reasons that fast-food packaging leaves a bad taste in our mouths. To prevent food from getting greasy and soggy, some fast-food companies coat their paper packaging with **per- and polyfluoroalkyl substances (PFAS)**, which are human-made chemicals used on everything from nonstick pans to stain-resistant clothing. PFAS are bad for the environment and human health.

WATER BOTTLES AND PLASTIC WASTE CLOG OUR OCEANS

Take a look at your watch and time 60 seconds. In that minute, more than a million bottles of water are being used around the world. About 38 billion plastic water bottles end up in US landfills per year. It wasn't that long ago—in the 1970s—that companies began selling bottled water. Nobody believed people would buy something you could easily get from a tap,

LIKE

SMART SOLUTIONS

Garbage from meal delivery adds up in other countries too. Kids as far away as the United Arab Emirates are also concerned about the waste created by our food-delivery habits. Students in Bahrain recently won an honorable mention in the Young Reporters for the Environment essay contest for their article about the topic. "With on-demand culture taking over the world, Bahrain too has jumped on the 'order in' bandwagon. However, is the convenience worth the cost?" they asked in their essay. After researching the issue from all sides, the students concluded: "There are plenty of smart solutions, however they require a new mentality which will sadly take time...all we can do as customers is to spread awareness and avoid online food delivery or use our own containers. It is our duty to hit the first domino to create the big change."

You might not think twice about drinking soda or water from a single-use plastic bottle, but all those bottles add up.
MAKIKO TANIGAWA/GETTY IMAGES

but they were wrong. Often they are ordered with fast food. And, of course, you can't forget plastic straws—Americans use about 400 million of them every day. Each straw takes 100 to 200 years to break down. Bottles and straws are called *single-use plastics*. Thanks to the pandemic that began in 2020, we use 250 to 300 percent more single-use plastic than we did before. Just think about how many disposable masks you used in a single day when the virus was at its peak. Lots of countries are trying to ban plastic straws and plastic bags, but it's still a huge problem.

You might be wondering why using so many plastic bottles is bad. After all, can't plastic be recycled? The truth is, a lot of plastic doesn't get recycled and ends up in the trash or washes up in oceans.

PRICE CHECK

In 2020, factories around the world produced 52 billion disposable face masks. Experts believe 1.6 billion of them ended up in the ocean. Because of health and safety rules, these things were nearly impossible to avoid. But now the planet has to deal with the mess.

And it never really disappears. Every piece of plastic ever made is still on Earth, even if it breaks down into microplastics.

Plastics and microplastics are bad news for animals too. Sea life can mistake microplastics for food and feed it to their babies, who can choke or get sick. Every year about 100,000 marine animals and about a million seabirds get caught in plastic and die. Sometimes plastic straws get stuck in turtles' noses. Microplastics also get absorbed by fish, which means your next tuna sandwich is not healthy to eat. In fact, one in three fish caught for people to eat contains plastic.

Experts think there could be millions or possibly even trillions of pieces of plastic in our oceans. If we don't do something about this problem, scientists warn, there will be more plastic in the oceans than fish.

People all over the world are getting together regularly to clean up their oceans and beaches.
WC.GI/GETTY IMAGES

PRICE CHECK

Surfers Against Sewage is a UK-based charity that focuses on protecting the world's oceans. Calling themselves "ocean activists," members organize beach cleanups, raise awareness about ocean pollution and work with governments to protect the oceans and marine life. They also conduct studies to find out which companies are the biggest polluters. Their 2022 study pointed a finger at the "Dirty Dozen"—12 companies that are currently responsible for 70 percent of our ocean waste, including single-use plastic bottles and plastic packaging. Coca-Cola and PepsiCo have been the top two highest-polluting companies for three years in a row. The Coca-Cola company's brands, which include Coca-Cola and Fanta, are responsible for 20 percent all on their own. Hopefully, by shining a light on these brands, it will force them to be accountable for their impact and lead them to do something about it.

SURFERS AGAINST SEWAGE

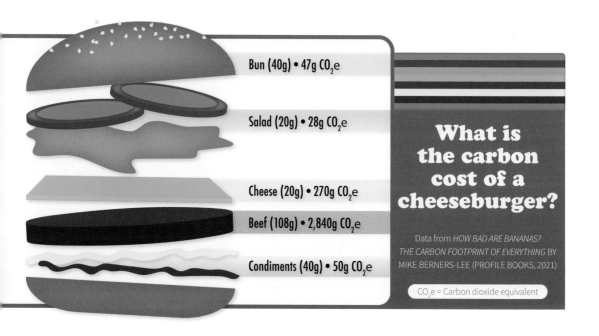

What is the carbon cost of a cheeseburger?

Bun (40g) • 47g CO_2e

Salad (20g) • 28g CO_2e

Cheese (20g) • 270g CO_2e

Beef (108g) • 2,840g CO_2e

Condiments (40g) • 50g CO_2e

Data from *HOW BAD ARE BANANAS? THE CARBON FOOTPRINT OF EVERYTHING* BY MIKE BERNERS-LEE (PROFILE BOOKS, 2021)

CO_2e = Carbon dioxide equivalent

LIKE

ANIMAL TREATMENT

To be sure you're eating healthier, more sustainable (responsibly produced) meat, seafood and dairy products, look for labels that say *free-range, cage-free, grass-fed, pasture-raised, animal welfare certified* or *organic*. Fish eaters can look for an Ocean Wise symbol or the blue Marine Stewardship Council seafood label. Of course, you probably don't buy your family's groceries, but next time you go with a grown-up to the store, take a look at the labels so you know what you're eating.

THE COST OF EATING MEAT

Fast food creates a lot of greenhouse gas emissions. These emissions happen when trees are cleared to make room for cattle, when grazing cattle pass gas, when meat is trucked to stores and restaurants and when cooked meat is delivered to your home.

By the time you unwrap your burger, it's made a big carbon footprint. Depending on the size of your patty, its carbon footprint could be about 100 ounces (2,840 grams) of CO_2 equivalent. Add the cheese, lettuce, tomato and bun, and the carbon footprint increases even more. Experts believe that emissions from food production, from vegetables to meat to milk, will use up 70 percent of the allowable greenhouse gas emissions by 2050. In other words, if humans are going to stop the world's temperatures from rising more than two degrees by 2050, we need to figure out how to reduce the impact of our food choices on the planet.

FAST FOOD CREATES FOOD WASTE

Every day almost one billion people go hungry while the rest of us throw away enough food to feed them. In fact, about a quarter to a third of the food produced around the world is wasted. We can all do a better job in our own homes, but when we go out to eat, food waste isn't all our fault. Many restaurants offer portions that are too big for us to eat. That's because people like to get good value for their money. Plus, plate sizes have grown so much in the last few decades that if we were served the right portions for our bodies, it would seem too small. We'd feel like we were being ripped off or underfed, even if we couldn't finish our food. Try not to order more than you can eat—or why not bring home leftovers for tomorrow's lunch?

ON THE MENU...SUSTAINABLE SOLUTIONS YOU CAN TRY AT HOME

TASTY NEW "MEAT" PRODUCTS

Have you noticed some new menu options at your favorite fast-food restaurant? Many restaurants are serving plant-based "meat" products like burgers, sausages and chicken nuggets. The production of real meat uses up varying amounts of land, which needs to be cleared to raise animals. Then the animals add greenhouse gas emissions to the air. But these new vegetarian and vegan items are made with ingredients like peas, potatoes, grains and tofu. Plant-based foods have a smaller carbon footprint than animal products do, and growing

PRICE CHECK

Global livestock production creates 7.8 billion tons (7.1 billion metric tons) of CO_2 a year—that's almost 15 percent of total worldwide emissions. How much is 15 percent? A lot!

them requires less land and water. One study even found that compared to beef burgers, plant-based burgers produced up to 98 percent less greenhouse gas emissions. Why not give them a try?

SAY "NO" TO SINGLE-USE PLASTIC PRODUCTS

I recently took my kids to McDonald's for a quick meal. As I waited for our food, I saw a poster on the counter. As part of its promise to do more for the planet, McDonald's Canada now offers compostable wooden forks and paper straws. By swapping wood for plastic, the chain prevents 925 tons (840 metric tons) of plastic from ending up in landfills per year. A lot of restaurants now use paper straws. Some even offer bamboo versions. I have reusable metal straws at home. Next time your family orders food for delivery online, let the restaurant know you don't need plastic cutlery. All you have to do to make an impact is click a button or tick a box. After all, you likely already have your own reusable cutlery at home.

Soon more and more restaurants won't be able to offer plastic cutlery even if customers forget to say no to it. That's because countries like Canada are banning single-use plastics. The federal government's goal is to achieve zero plastic waste by 2030 to reduce greenhouse gas emissions. Some restaurants and grocery stores are getting ahead of the laws and using things like paper bags instead of plastic.

COURTESY OF SOPHIA MATHUR

USE BETTER ALTERNATIVES

Landfills everywhere are packed with takeout coffee cups. Billions of these nonrecyclable cups end up in our oceans

 THE STRAW THAT BROKE THE CAMEL'S BACK

Sophia Mathur is a teen from Sudbury, Ontario. She was just seven when she began standing up for the planet. She's so passionate about the environment that in 2018 she was the first student outside Europe to walk out of class as part of the *Fridays for Future* movement to demand action on climate change. Mathur also participated in the Last Plastic Straw Movement, convincing local restaurants and bars to put a fork in their use of plastic straws. In May 2019 Sudbury's city council declared a *climate emergency* and pledged to achieve net-zero emissions by 2050. Other kids around the world are also taking action and telling restaurants to quit using single-use plastics. Sisters Amy and Ella Meek from the United Kingdom co-founded Kids Against Plastic when they were 12 and 10 respectively. They have picked up more than 90,000 pieces of single-use plastic garbage and convinced 1,000 schools and 50 cafés, businesses and festivals to join their fight against plastic pollution. Then there's Milo Cress from the United States. In 2011, when he was nine years old, he started the Be Straw Free campaign to get straw makers, restaurants, schools and everyday straw users to stop using disposable plastic straws. He was upset to learn that Americans use 500 million straws every day—enough to fill more than 125 large school buses. Success tastes sweet—especially when you can drink it without a plastic straw.

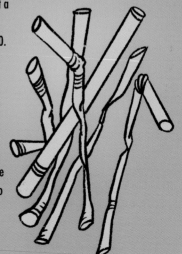

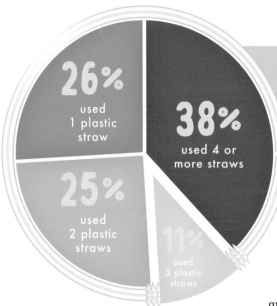

26% used 1 plastic straw

38% used 4 or more straws

25% used 2 plastic straws

11% used 3 plastic straws

HOW MANY PLASTIC STRAWS DO YOU USE IN A WEEK?

One study asked Canadians how many plastic straws they use in an average week. Here's what the survey showed.

Coffee grounds can be reused to make things like scrubs and candles, and they can be used in your garden too.
WACHIWIT/GETTY IMAGES

and landfills each year. And what about the coffee grounds? Even though they can be composted and turned into rich garden fertilizer, millions of tons of coffee grounds are tossed in the trash annually. When they decompose in a landfill, coffee grounds release methane gas, so it's better for the planet to keep grounds out of the trash. Your parents or guardians don't have to kick caffeine to the curb. You can remind them to bring a reusable cup to their local coffee shop and compost their spent grounds when they make coffee at home. Your local Starbucks might even offer Grounds for Your Garden. In some locations the coffee chain gives away used coffee grounds to customers who want to compost them at home.

Companies are also finding new ways to upcycle coffee grounds. Did you know they can be used to make everything from coffee-scented candles to bath and body products? I like buying coffee scrubs made with grounds. Some places even sell these beauty products "naked," without any packaging. A company called Nudge sells "coffee bombs" in little tin containers so your parents can get their caffeine without a cup. And in England's Premier League, the Manchester City Football Club sells coffee in edible cups made from leakproof wafers. Fans can drink their coffee and then eat the cup. It's all part of the soccer team's commitment to finding sustainable ways to manage waste created at their sporting events.

MAKE YOUR OWN "FAST FOOD"

Before ordering in or going out, see what kinds of "fast food" you can make at home. Start by looking in your fridge. Before your cheese, pepperoni or vegetables go bad, think of ways you can use them all up rather than buying more ingredients at the store. Try a make-your-own pizza or taco night. There's actually lots you can do with ingredients you already have on hand. You can make chocolate pudding with milk approaching its best-before date. Or chicken salad if you have leftover roast chicken, wilting celery or even grapes. If you have fruit, freeze it and throw it in a smoothie another day. Or blend it to make popsicles.

COURTESY OF JULIANNA GRECO

Julianna Greco loves ordering takeout food, but she felt bad about doing it. "Toronto serves about 39 million takeout meals per year, which means we are tossing more than 78 million pieces of waste each year," says Greco. "The numbers are staggering."

Lots of people like ordering takeout. But there's a big problem with the containers—most of them aren't recycled. "In Canada, only 9 percent of everything we throw away actually gets recycled," says Greco. "A large majority ends up in landfills, where it creates landfill gas, made of methane and carbon dioxide. Both are contributors [to] global warming. Switching to reusable containers is a good way to solve that."

With Megan Takeda-Tully, Greco cofounded a company called Suppli, which provides eco-minded restaurants with reusable stainless-steel takeout containers. When customers order food, it's served in these environmentally friendly, leakproof alternatives to plastic and Styrofoam. When people are done with their containers, they return them at nearby drop-off locations. Greco's goal is to help the restaurant industry say goodbye to single-use containers for good while also building awareness for the reuse movement.

Within a year of launching, the company had partnered with more than 25 local restaurants, from Thai to Venezuelan, and saved about 10,000 single-use takeout containers from the landfill. Greco and Takeda-Tully plan to expand across Canada and beyond in the coming years. "We get email requests from all over the world, from Japan to Hawaii, asking us to start Suppli in their area," she says. "Consumers and businesses were waiting for this and want it to happen. I hope future generations will wonder what a single-use takeout container was!"

SUPER

SAVER

MEET THE COFOUNDER OF A REUSABLE REVOLUTION

In the meantime, Greco offers her top three tips for readers concerned about fast-food waste:

- Skip some stuff—when ordering takeout, ask restaurants not to provide you with cutlery or condiments. Usually you have these things at home anyway.
- Bring your own food-storage containers and ask restaurants to use them. Even if you're picking up hamburgers, it doesn't hurt to ask.
- Do your own garbage analysis. Look at everything in your garbage and recycling bins. What takes up the most space in your bin? Try to reduce it.

Two women in Brooklyn, New York, make pizza using *"ugly" vegetables*—the veggies that look a little funny or misshapen. They also use vegetables or parts of veggies (like broccoli leaves and carrot tops) that are delicious and nutritious but can't be sold by farms or stores. These ugly vegetables or leftover parts can be chopped, blended and cooked to make sauce or be used as toppings.

"Forty percent of all food in the US is wasted daily," says Jane Katz, cofounder with Jessica Smith of Scraps Pizza. "We started Scraps to do something about this. We create the most delicious frozen pizza out there, and we set out to reduce waste by incorporating imperfect and underused veggies in our sauces." Their green pizza is made with broccoli leaves, which are blended into their green sauce. Their red pizzas use ugly but yummy red peppers.

The co-founders of Scraps Pizza use up all their veggie scraps to make delicious sauces and toppings for their pizzas.
COURTESY OF JANE KATZ

CHOP YOUR FAMILY'S FOOD WASTE

If everyone around the world cut their food waste in half, we'd prevent 1.8 billion tons (1.63 billion metric tons) of carbon emissions. You and your family can easily slice and dice your own food waste at home. Here are a few ideas:

X EAT LEFTOVERS PROMPTLY OR FREEZE THEM FOR ANOTHER DAY.

X ASK FOR DOGGIE BAGS IF YOU CAN'T FINISH YOUR RESTAURANT FOOD.

X ONLY TAKE WHAT YOU CAN EAT. HAVE MORE IF YOU'RE STILL HUNGRY.

- [X] LOOK IN YOUR FRIDGE AND PANTRY BEFORE YOU SHOP. TAKE A LIST TO THE STORE SO YOU DON'T BUY THINGS YOU ALREADY HAVE.

- [X] BEST-BEFORE DATES CAN BE MISLEADING. THEY DON'T ALWAYS TELL YOU WHEN FOOD IS BAD OR UNSAFE TO EAT. BEFORE THROWING AWAY "EXPIRED" FOODS, SMELL YOUR FOOD OR CHECK FOR SIGNS OF MOLD.

- [X] YOU CAN FIGHT MORE THAN FOOD WASTE AT HOME. USE A STAINLESS-STEEL LUNCH BOX OR REUSABLE CONTAINERS SO YOU DON'T NEED PLASTIC BAGS OR CLING WRAP.

- ✳ AVOID INDIVIDUALLY WRAPPED FOODS, LIKE PACKAGED COOKIES AND GRANOLA BARS. INSTEAD TRY MAKING YOUR OWN.

LIKE

⦿ CHEFS COOK UP CHANGE

Chef Adam Smith is dedicated to "feeding bellies, not bins." He founded the Real Junk Food Project in Leeds, UK, in 2013. The project rescues food that's about to be thrown out by grocery stores, restaurants, farms and other places. Instead of letting this good food go to waste, Smith uses these ingredients to make delicious meals at his café. People who can't pay for their food can help clean up. The price for people who can afford it? Pay as you feel. The concept has become a big movement. It's spread to places like Manchester, Bristol, Los Angeles, Brazil, Warsaw and Zurich.

Other chefs are doing their part too. The Edible Schoolyard was started over 25 years ago by Alice Waters in Berkeley, California. The chef, author and activist is helping give public-school students a more hands-on "edible education" by using organic school gardens to teach kids about nutrition and sustainability. After all, as the nonprofit organization points out, good food should be a right, not a privilege.

Many other chefs, nonprofit organizations and activists, from New York to Rome, are also working with schools to teach kids about the connection between what we eat and the health of our planet. By composting, growing gardens, serving nutritious local foods and doing away with single-use plastics, they are helping develop smart, sustainable habits in people from a young age.

CHAPTER THREE

You Used to Call Me

If you like the latest technology, put up your hand. Okay, you don't actually have to do that—you can use the thumbs-up emoji. The truth is, I like having the newest-model phone and a lightning-fast laptop computer. And so do a lot of other people, it seems. More than 5 billion people use smartphones—that's about two-thirds of the entire global population.

But when a new model comes out, what happens to the gadgets we've been using? Most of them end up in the dump. In China alone, 750 million electronic devices are thrown away every year. Americans produce up to 7.6 million tons (6.9 million metric tons) of tech trash a year—that's more than the combined weight of every blue whale in the ocean. Some say the average American

We throw away millions of cell phones each year, but there are ways to make them last longer. Many can be reused or recycled.
ROMAN MYKHALCHUK/GETTY IMAGES

keeps their cell phone for only 34 months before getting a new one. Others estimate that we keep our phones for just 18 months.

You might wonder why this is a big deal. After all, isn't progress good? And can't computers and phones be recycled? The answer is yes...and no. Eventually the majority of these devices become **e-waste**, a term for all the old electronics that are no longer wanted or have become obsolete, from phones, laptops and gaming systems to tablets, televisions and photocopiers. One report found that although e-waste makes up just 2 percent of the waste in American landfills, it creates over 70 percent of the country's toxic garbage. The fact is, most of the time we don't or can't recycle e-waste properly, which has consequences for the planet and people.

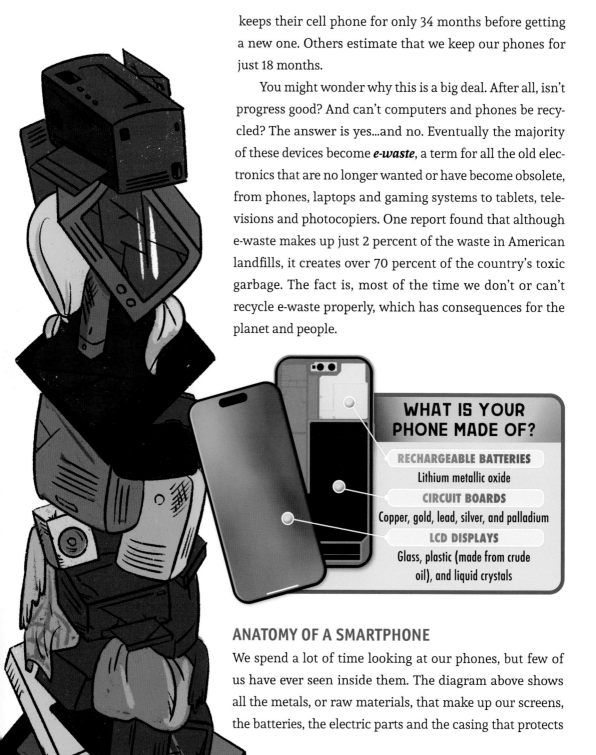

WHAT IS YOUR PHONE MADE OF?

RECHARGEABLE BATTERIES
Lithium metallic oxide

CIRCUIT BOARDS
Copper, gold, lead, silver, and palladium

LCD DISPLAYS
Glass, plastic (made from crude oil), and liquid crystals

ANATOMY OF A SMARTPHONE

We spend a lot of time looking at our phones, but few of us have ever seen inside them. The diagram above shows all the metals, or raw materials, that make up our screens, the batteries, the electric parts and the casing that protects everything inside. Even without reading the chart, we can see that a lot of metals go into making our phones. All those materials are mined from the earth. We might love our phones, but when they end up in the dump, things begin to get glitchy.

THE PROBLEM WITH E-WASTE

Sure, electronic devices can be recycled when we're done with them. But look at this chart on the right. See all the red boxes? Those are all the elements that are recycled less than 1 percent of the time. Even the green boxes are metals that get recycled only about half the time. That's because it's not easy to take apart phones and separate all the metals. It's time-consuming, and there aren't a lot of places that recycle devices properly—or at all. A lot of the time, we just chuck our old phones in a drawer or throw them away. We don't think to recycle them the way we recycle soda cans. So things like our old printers, TVs, microwaves and cameras end up in the landfill. When they pile up in the dump, along with wasted food, dirty diapers, clothes, Styrofoam and whatever else we toss away, all those metals leach harmful chemicals into our soil and water supply. It's bad news for the planet—and for us.

HOW E-WASTE IMPACTS THE PLANET

THE GROUND AND WATER

Think about how you would feel in this scenario. You're playing football with your friends on a sunny summer day. You are going for a touchdown, but your friends catch up to you and tackle you to the ground. You're on the bottom as they all pile on top of you—and they stay there until the

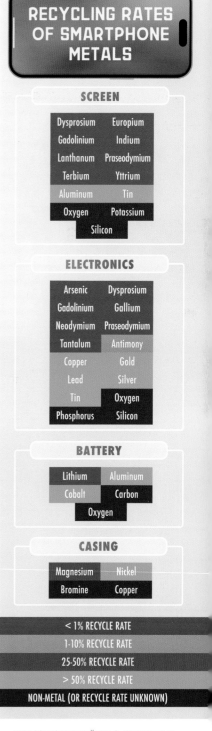

DATA SOURCE: HAGELÜKEN, C., GOLDMANN, D. *RECYCLING AND CIRCULAR ECONOMY—TOWARDS A CLOSED LOOP FOR METALS IN EMERGING CLEAN TECHNOLOGIES.* MINER ECON 35, 539–562 (2022).

referee blows her whistle. You'd probably get very hot under that heap of sweaty players. The same thing happens to our e-waste when it's in a landfill—it heats up. When e-waste is warmed up, toxic chemicals from the metal parts ooze out and contaminate our soil and water. If fish or other marine life come into contact with poisonous water, they can get sick and die. And if humans eat those fish, we can get sick too. If we accidentally eat lead, for example, it can damage our blood, kidneys and nervous systems.

PRICE CHECK

Making phones produces greenhouse gas emissions. Approximately 200 pounds (about 91 kilograms) of CO_2 are created every time a cell phone is made. Here's how:

- About 43 percent of the CO_2 created or used during the life of a cell phone is emitted during the raw material phase. This is thanks to the machines needed to find, remove and refine the petroleum that makes plastic and mine the metals needed for batteries and circuit boards. These machines use gasoline or diesel fuel, both of which release greenhouse gases.

- About 34 percent is created during manufacturing by factories using electricity, which tends to be generated by *fossil fuels* like coal and natural gas.

- Nine percent of the CO_2 is created during distribution by the trucks that deliver the phones to stores. They also use gas and diesel when they drive.

- Eleven percent of CO_2 is created to produce the electricity used to recharge our phone batteries again and again.

- Disposal/resell/recycle. The final one percent is created when we get rid of our phones after we're finished using them.

THE AIR

Sometimes, instead of rotting in a landfill, garbage is burned. When e-waste is in the pile and metals like copper, aluminum and iron are set on fire, poisonous chemicals fill the air. Countries around the world send toxic e-waste to a place called Guiyu, China, for disposal. It's the largest e-waste disposal site in China and maybe even the world. Researchers decided to measure air quality in the area. It contained so many polybrominated diphenyl ethers (PBDEs) that the air was 140 times more toxic than in Hong Kong. When the air is filled with such high amounts of poison, it can make people and animals ill and heat up the planet in the process. Many people who live in Guiyu are reported to have health problems, including digestive, brain, breathing and bone issues.

Electronics are burned at disposal sites, causing poisonous gases to pollute the air and water.

JORDAN LYE/GETTY IMAGES

LIKE

RECYCLING IS A GOOD IDEA!

If we recycled the 1.5 billion cell phones bought each year, we wouldn't need to mine so many precious metals from the earth. This is what we would save:

105,000 pounds (47,600 kilograms) of gold (worth $123 billion)

1.5 million pounds (476,000 kilograms) of silver (about the same weight as 680 cars)

46.3 million pounds (21 million kilograms) of copper (the same amount of copper as 750 Statues of Liberty)

0.77 million pounds (35 million kilograms) of aluminum (about the same weight as 7,800 elephants)

45

THE HUMAN TOLL

You just read about the people in Guiyu and the toll e-waste takes on their health. But millions of other people are impacted too—including kids your age. The **World Health Organization (WHO)** says that as many as 12.9 million women are combing through piles of e-waste to separate all the valuable metals from the plastic. More than 18 million children and teens, some as young as five, also help with e-waste recycling. If they can separate the metals and sell the pieces, they earn a little bit of money to help feed their families. Picking through e-waste exposes people in developing countries to chemicals that can damage their brains and other parts of their bodies.

Child labor is also an issue, especially in poorer countries with unstable governments and laws that don't protect workers' or children's rights. It's estimated that more than one million **child laborers**, some as young as six or seven, work in mines and quarries to find the metals we need for our phones. Instead of going to school or playing on the playground, they risk their lives by working in unsafe mines where they breathe in thick clouds of deadly dust. Some might get paid only one or two dollars a day for their work. They have no choice—if they don't work, they can face violence, intimidation or worse.

Cobalt is used in our electronic devices and electric car batteries to make them run. Unfortunately, mining cobalt comes at a cost.

RHJ/GETTY IMAGES

NO COBALT, NO CALLS

We can't send an email, make a TikTok video or even drive an electric car without cobalt, a valuable mineral that's only found deep in mines and needed to make all rechargeable lithium batteries. Demand for precious minerals is only increasing, along with our appetite for new technology. More than 60 percent of the world's supply of cobalt comes from mines in the Democratic Republic of the Congo. About 40,000 children work in mines in that country, some as young as six years old. Human rights groups are raising awareness and holding big tech companies accountable for their practices. Meanwhile, some companies have stepped up and put practices in place to ensure that mining is safer, more ethical and sustainable.

SOLUTIONS AROUND THE WORLD

E-waste has been called one of the "largest and most complex waste streams in the world." That's why many organizations, including governments, the WHO and the United Nations, as well as people like you and me, are trying to help. Here are a few examples of things happening all over the world:

Japan takes e-waste seriously. Tech makers and users are responsible for disposing of gadgets properly. Laws ensure that manufacturers of computers and appliances, for instance, provide proper recycling facilities. Another law requires consumers to pay to ship and recycle their e-waste.

India was once the world's fifth-largest e-waste producer, dumping or burning 95 percent of its electronics. But the UN trained more than 2,000 waste pickers to collect, recycle and dispose of e-waste more safely. Recycling companies are now required to pay workers more money for the metals they find. Today more than 18.7 tons (17 metric tons) of e-waste is collected each year and about 20 percent is recycled.

People in India pick through the garbage to collect e-waste so it can be properly disposed of.
DIPAK SHELARE/SHUTTERSTOCK.COM

In 2009 Martine Postma organized the first repair café in Amsterdam. It's a place where people can bring broken electrical appliances like phones—and even furniture and bicycles—to get them repaired. Now these cafés have popped up in over 100 cities around the world. A poll found that about 80 percent of Europeans would rather repair their devices than replace them. And most think that manufacturers should be legally responsible for helping people do it. Those little cafés helped lead Europeans to ask why their appliances and gadgets are so hard to repair. It turns out manufacturers don't keep spare parts, and they use special tools that most people don't have at home. Sometimes products even break when you try to open them—they're designed that way on purpose! And without manuals, things like fridges and dishwashers are impossible to fix. It's caused people to throw away things that actually can be repaired. Fortunately this is starting to change. Right to Repair laws in parts of Europe are ensuring that manufacturers carry spare parts, use common tools and provide manuals so people can fix products on their own.

New laws are making it easier for students just like these to fix products thanks to online instructions and parts that are easier to buy.
IFIXIT

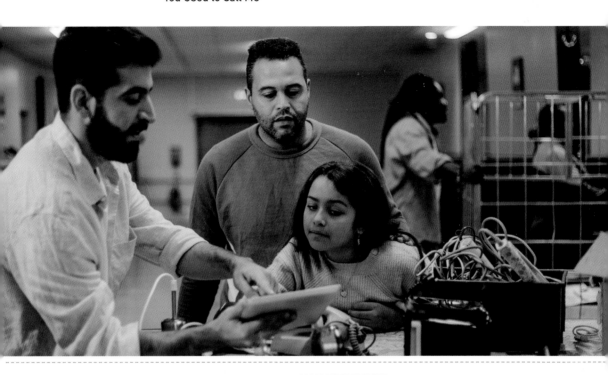

To tackle its e-waste, France unveiled an anti-waste law in 2020 that includes providing people with repairability ratings for goods, on a scale of 1 to 10. The government is encouraging manufacturers to design products that are easier to open and fix. The government's goal is that by 2026, 60 percent of electronic equipment will be repairable.

In North America, the repair-law movement hasn't taken off in the same way. So millions of do-it-yourselfers rely on an online community called iFixit for help repairing gadgets. Started in California and used worldwide, iFixit provides free step-by-step instructions, in 11 languages, for more than 80,000 products. When we can fix products instead of replacing them, we help create jobs, reduce the need to mine for metals and produce less e-waste.

Going to a repair café is a great way to get products fixed instead of throwing them away.
MASKOT/GETTY IMAGES

Companies like Fairphone make products that are easy to repair—and they're letting people know where all the parts come from.

OVKNHR/SHUTTERSTOCK.COM

Erin Silver

Fairphone is a Dutch company dedicated to protecting workers' rights, using materials responsibly and reducing e-waste. Unlike many big tech companies, Fairphone is open about its supply chain—the company knows where all its materials come from, who makes them and under what conditions. It's all mapped out on the Fairphone website. Fairphones last longer and are easier to repair than other brands, and they can be recycled when they're truly not usable anymore. Unfortunately, they're available only in Europe. German company Shift also makes phones that are repairable and produced in a way that's fair to workers and the environment. There are even video repair guides on the company's website so users can fix everything from the Shiftphone's camera to its screen.

The Framework laptop is a high-performance notebook computer that's easy to upgrade and repair. Available in several countries, including the United States, France and Australia, there are even DIY editions you can build yourself. Upgrade kits come with QR codes that are linked to repair manuals and sold with the screwdriver you need to put your computer together. It's known as the most repairable product on the market.

Research engineers working in labs, not mines, are finding new ways to 3D-print phone parts—parts made of materials that don't easily shatter, aren't made of metal and are easier to recycle. They're even finding new materials that would enable batteries to last longer. If experts can find ways to replace precious metals with better alternatives, it will have a positive impact on the planet.

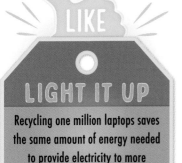

LIKE

LIGHT IT UP

Recycling one million laptops saves the same amount of energy needed to provide electricity to more than 3,500 US homes in a year.

Most phone companies don't want people to fix their phones. After all, their job is to sell you the latest and greatest. But they are still under pressure to make changes. Apple, for example, launched a repair program for small businesses. These small fix-it shops get things like Apple parts, tools and training so they can fix devices no longer under warranty. (A warranty is a guarantee that for a specified amount of time after purchase, a company will repair or replace a defective device.)

PRICE CHECK

If we kept our phones for eight months longer than we usually would, we could cut CO_2 emissions by about 38 million tons (35 million metric tons)—the same amount of CO_2 emissions created by Ireland every year.

HERE'S HOW KIDS AND ORGANIZATIONS ARE HELPING

The cofounder of iFixit, Kyle Wiens, visited a school in Yukon in 2022. He challenged the teens to learn how to repair a cracked phone screen in an hour. Guess what? They all did it! The challenge was filmed for a CBC documentary called *Curb Your Carbon*. If we're going to improve the future of the planet, Wiens says we need to make things last as long as possible. Why not start a repair club at home or invite a guest to show your class how to fix your gadgets? It would be a great idea for International E-Waste Day on October 14!

Nonprofit organizations like Computers4Kids in Charlottesville, Virginia, get computer donations from businesses and families and fix them up for kids. When computers can't be repaired, after-school programs teach kids how to use those parts to make new products.

Google launched a Chromebook repair program for schools in the United States. Since Chromebooks are used by 50 million students and teachers—and can easily fall off desks and slip out of backpacks—the company created a way for students to start their own repair programs. Inspired by Jenks Public Schools in Oklahoma, whose in-school repair service led to speedier Chromebook repairs and graduates with strong IT skills, Google created a "playbook" with lots of resources for schools.

Dell Technologies partnered with Goodwill, a nonprofit organization that provides job training and community-based programs for people in need. Since 2004, people across North America can drop off their old technology at a Goodwill center, and Dell ensures that it's all recycled properly. Thousands of jobs have been created through the Dell Reconnect program, and billions of pounds of e-waste have been diverted from landfills.

LIKE

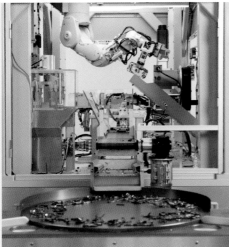

● MEET DAISY

After years of research, Apple introduced Liam in 2016—the first robot that could take apart iPhones to recover valuable parts. Liam couldn't keep up with the number of phones that needed disassembly, and it could only take apart the iPhone 6. So Apple invented Daisy. She can take apart 23 models of the iPhone and sort their high-quality pieces for recycling. Around the world, Apple makes it easy to send in used devices. They will refurbish or recycle them for free, and in some countries, you'll even get an Apple credit as thanks.

APPLE

Recycling depots like this help properly dispose of e-waste.
MASSIMO BORCHI, ATLANTIDE PHOTOTRAVEL/GETTY IMAGES

LIKE

YOU CAN DO IT

I was cleaning out my garage and had an old TV I wanted to recycle. I was happy to find a site called RecycleMyElectronics.ca. It helps you find a recycling depot near you. You can also arrange for a pickup. If your family needs to recycle e-waste, go online to find similar sites that can guide you in the right direction.

Homeboy Industries' mission is to help improve the lives of men and women who were previously in prison or in gangs. One of its training programs is called Homeboy Electronics Recycling. This award-winning company trains employees to repair, resell or recycle electronic equipment. For every 75,000 pounds (34,019 kilograms) of electronic equipment that's donated to the program, Homeboy Industries can create a new job. People who need a new computer can stop by one of the Homeboy retail stores and buy one at a reasonable price.

SAVER

MAKE YOUR TECHNOLOGY LAST LONGER

It all began when Jessa Jones's toddlers flushed her phone down the toilet. Before she knew it, she had ripped the toilet out of the bathroom and smashed it open with a sledgehammer to find her phone. She then figured out how to fix the phone herself, and with her new expertise, she started a business in her dining room, repairing other people's phones.

I spoke to Jones, owner of iPad Rehab in Honeoye, New York, for expert advice on how to extend the life of your devices.

What are your top five tips for kids who want their devices to last a long time?

> You don't want to break your phone. Today they're harder for kids to fix. Here are my five best tips.

TIP 1: The way kids break their devices is through carelessness. My daughters sit on the floor when they use their devices, and they often leave their iPad on the floor. It leads to [an iPad] getting stepped on. Make a designated spot for it to go. Never leave it on the floor. Try to keep it away from water, drinks, etc.

TIP 2: There are different types of chargers for your devices. The one that came with your device has a circuit board that will help protect it. If you lose that charger and get another, the new one can be hit or miss. There are lots of inexpensive chargers out there, but they don't protect your phone from electrical damage or power surges. You could be at risk of frying your device. Having a high-quality charger is important to prolonging the life of your device.

TIP 3: If your phone gets wet, don't put the phone in rice. The idea that rice is helpful is not true. It's a myth. Dry rice doesn't absorb water. When water gets inside electronics, it will eventually evaporate if you do nothing and leave it on the counter.

If you open the device up, you could accelerate drying by using paper towel to dab at it. Sometimes when water gets in, it will cause a short circuit and no amount of drying will help.

TIP 4: Get in the habit of backing up your information while you're young because it becomes really important as an adult. Have iCloud storage and set your phone to back up automatically. If you have an Android, you can back up your data to Google Photos. You can also plug your phone into a computer regularly and tell it to back up to the computer. Make sure to give your password to a trusted adult or friend, just in case you forget.

TIP 5: You can use tempered glass to protect your screen, but there's no hard evidence that it definitely protects your phone. It can crack. Having a case is probably a good idea for kids who want to have a phone for the long term.

What if your phone doesn't work?

Kids are always attracted to the newer phone. But there are things you can do when your phone doesn't work. The first thing I'd do is go to a trusted local repair shop. If you go to a big-box store, they will try to sell you a new one. It's how they stay in business.

How long should devices last?

You should get five years out of your phone for sure. For laptops, at least five years is a reasonable target. If you notice your battery is running out quickly, you can replace the battery. That might happen on year two, and then it will be good for another solid chunk of time. You can also replace charge cords on gaming consoles, for instance. A local repair shop can open it and put a new charge cord in or HDMI port.

When should you get a new one?

It depends on what you use it for. In general, the hardware inside a device is like an engine. When it's brand new and top of the line, it's going to have an engine that runs today's software. Over time software gets updated, and it becomes harder for the engine to keep up with the heavier load of software. Eventually you will have a hardware-software mismatch. Your phone will really slow down and crash, it won't be able to load software, and it can't be updated.

Then what do you do with your old devices?

By the time a device truly gets to the point where it's time for a new one, it won't have any value in the United States or Canada. There are electronic recycling companies that are certified to recycle devices. If they don't give you any value for it, it's a sign you've done a good job. If they give you money for it, it means they intend to repair and sell it. It has value because it can be fixed.

CHAPTER FOUR

Gifts Galore

Getting the right gifts for friends and family can be hard. The options are endless. A plastic gift card is convenient and considerate—people can buy what they want. When you were younger, you probably gave and received toys. You know, those plastic action figures, dolls or games that came in plastic-wrapped boxes and were handed to you in wrapping paper that you threw in the trash. Now, even though you're older, you probably still get excited during the holidays or on your birthday when someone hands you a wrapped present. It's also fun to get the kind of toys that come in a loot bag—colorful squishy toys, fidget spinners or stress balls.

Unfortunately, many of these gifts aren't made sustainably. Even those little plastic gift cards are bad for

We love giving and receiving gifts, but how can we make gifting more sustainable?
RUSS ROHDE/GETTY IMAGES

the planet. This chapter "unwraps" the problem with gifting and shows how you can give **sustainable gifts**, including some thoughtful, carbon-free presents you can make yourself.

FROM THE PAST TO THE "PRESENT"

Gift giving is a tradition in many cultures around the world. It makes the recipient feel special, and studies show that it makes the giver feel happier too. It's also a good way to express yourself or tell someone something without saying a word.

Giving people presents has been popular since humans existed. Early humans gave teeth and stones to show affection and prove they could take care of their families. Those teeth and stones were carved to be strung on necklaces, which were shown off to other early humans. Ancient Egyptians get credit for giving the first birthday gifts—food, jewelry and bowls. Books, manuscripts and even love songs

Gift giving in ancient times meant that people gave one another things like teeth, stone carvings and food.
NIALL O DONOGHUE/DREAMSTIME.COM

were popular gifts in the Middle Ages. People also started giving wedding gifts, usually things like cows, money and property. China may have been the first country to popularize wrapping paper, and in the Chinese tradition, people still give New Year's gifts wrapped in red paper for luck.

In the 1800s holiday gift giving became big business. Typical Christmas presents back then were coal, candy and toys. When my grandparents were kids, they would have played with handmade dolls packed with feathers or cloth, or teddy bears stuffed with sawdust. Popular toys were soldiers made of lead and marbles made of clay, stone or glass. Wooden blocks, electric trains and homemade board games were hits when my parents were growing up. But by the time I was a kid, factories were able to make bright new toys on the cheap, which meant there was always something I wanted at the toy store. My siblings and I had a lot of plastic toys—everything from LEGO sets to Barbies to wrestling action figures. You probably play with toys too—remote-control cars, race track sets and stuffies. What's one thing these kinds of toys have in common? They all contain plastic.

A DANGER TO OUR HEALTH

There's a problem with plastic toys made in certain countries—many contain harmful chemicals, such as **phthalates**, **polyvinyl chloride (PVC)** and **bisphenol A (BPA)**. Substances like these make plastics hard, colorful, soft or flexible. They've also been linked to cancer, birth defects, learning difficulties and other illnesses. The issue is so big that during the 2018 holiday shopping season, European parents were advised not to buy plastic toys. Too many were made with illegal chemicals. Then a safety investigation found that half of the slime and

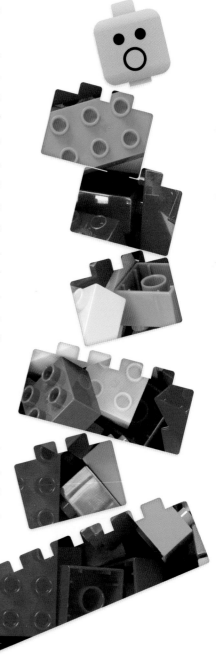

Plastic toys may come with some health risks, depending what you buy and when you bought it.
WAKILA/GETTY IMAGES

59

Look for symbols like these when buying toys for younger kids. They indicate that the product is safe.

VLADIMIR IVANKIN/GETTY IMAGES

EULALIA CAYUELA MARTINEZ/GETTY IMAGES

MENSENT PHOTOGRAPHY/ GETTY IMAGES

putty on UK store shelves was unsafe. It had too much boron, which can cause diarrhea and vomiting and even affect reproductive organs. That year was a difficult toy-shopping season in Denmark, too. The country banned soft foam "squishes" after inspectors found they were made with cancer-causing chemicals.

So what are the best toys to buy a little kid? Traditional books or cloth books are a safe bet. Shop for products that say *BPA-free* on the label or buy toys made of solid wood, organic fabric or natural rubber. Don't buy anything that smells like plastic or has flaking paint. And while it's great for the environment to donate your old toys, some contain **semivolatile organic compounds**—chemicals that can release dangerous toxins for 15 years or longer.

A PROBLEM FOR THE PLANET

Plastic gifts aren't good for human health, and they're bad for the planet too. Here are some of the top reasons why:

THEY END UP IN THE LANDFILL

Most plastic toys are cheap and colorful. We get them in cereal boxes, at fairs, parties and even at fast-food chains and dentists' offices. They make up 90 percent of toys on the market. Kids get bored with them quickly, and they break easily. And in a poll conducted by the British Heart Foundation, more than 25 percent of parents admitted they throw away toys that aren't even broken. Because many plastic toys contain other materials, like lead, recycling companies can't separate the plastic parts from the metal, which means they are taken to the dump.

EVEN GIFT CARDS CAN'T BE RECYCLED

In 2020 the average shopper in the United States bought almost 28 gift cards. Globally people spent $295.2 billion US on gift cards. Experts predict that number will rise to $440.7 billion by the end of 2028. Most gift cards are thrown away after the money on the card is spent. And most are made of PVC, a single-use plastic that's nondegradable, which means it can exist forever in a landfill, releasing cancer-causing toxins and other pollutants into the air and ground. That's why PVC is considered the most environmentally damaging plastic ever created. A single plastic gift card contains about 0.17 ounces (5 grams) of PVC (roughly the weight of a sheet of paper) and generates 0.74 ounces (21 grams) of CO_2 (that's about the weight of a double-A battery).

Plus, half of American adults forget to use their gift cards. The good news is, you can buy e-gift cards instead. Economists expect the popularity of digital gift cards to increase by 23 percent by 2025. That could be good news for you too, as you're less likely to forget to use a e-gift card that's on your phone.

If you've received a plastic card, ask the store if it takes back empty gift cards to reuse. Or look online for a company near you that recycles PVC.

PACKAGING AND WRAPPING

One of the big problems with toys is that they come with lots of packaging—packaging that's meant to be thrown out and can't easily be recycled.

PRICE CHECK

Some toys are a safety hazard. In 2015 so many hoverboards caught fire that 10 companies recalled more than 500,000 of these electronic skateboards. Before that, in the late 1990s, Fisher-Price had to recall 10 million ride-on trucks and cars after these battery-powered toys were also called a fire hazard. A nonprofit organization called World Against Toys Causing Harm (W.A.T.C.H.) publishes an annual list of the 10 worst toys. The most dangerous toy for 2022 was a musical learning watch. Its battery could cause chemical burns and death if ingested.

KAZATIN/GETTY IMAGES

PRICE CHECK

In 2022 gift-card sales in the United States totaled $189 billion. It's a problem, since experts say 10 billion new gift cards are created every year, adding 75 to 100 million pounds (34 to 45 million kilograms) of PVC to landfills annually. What are physical gift cards made from? The same harmful PVC as credit cards and hotel keys.

Just think about the typical action figure or doll that comes in a box with a plastic window and is fastened in place by wire twist ties, metal screws, plastic bags or elastics. These parts are so difficult to sort that the whole thing ends up in the landfill. The problem is especially noticeable after the holidays. Garbage collectors in Edmonton, for example, say the amount of plastic packaging put out to curb doubles at that time. The City of Edmonton created an app called WasteWise to help people sort their waste. Many other cities have done the same, but it doesn't fix the problem if people don't sort their waste properly. When shopping, try to choose items with as little packaging as possible.

WE HAVE TOO MUCH

It's hard to disagree with the idea that people in wealthy countries have too much. One study in the UK involving 2,000 parents found that kids have about four toys they've never even played with. It's so out of hand that a nursery school in Bristol, UK, got back to basics. For one month they put all their toys in another room and gave the kids things like cardboard boxes, tins and pretend paper train tickets instead. Teachers, parents and kids loved the experiment. Staff found that children went outdoors more, talked more and played more. They were even more creative. "A box becomes a spaceship, a stick becomes a wand, they become a wizard," one parent told the BBC in an interview. "My little boy Oliver has been loving it." The school proved you don't need tons of toys to have a lot of fun.

Kids don't need plastic toys in order to use their imaginations, so why do we continue to create and buy so many?
RON LEVINE/GETTY IMAGES

PRICE CHECK

People spend a lot of money on gifts others don't want. Between American Thanksgiving and New Year's Day, the waste produced by families jumps about 25 percent, totaling about an extra million tons (about 0.9 million metric tons) of trash a week. What can you do with gifts you don't want? Donate them. Or ask your friends and family what they want in advance.

CAUSING A BUYING FRENZY

Do you have a favorite gift? Here's a look back at some of the most popular gifts of all time. No matter how much people loved them, guess where these gifts probably are now? Do you notice anything else they all have in common?

1978

Whose hippo could eat more plastic marbles in a game of Hungry Hungry Hippos? Kids had a big appetite for this game when it was new.

1936

Monopoly, the real-estate board game, still turns kids into tycoons.

1943

The Slinky could walk down stairs…or could it?

1980

Rubik's Cube is the 3D combination puzzle that's just as challenging to solve today as it was back then.

1952

Mr. Potato Head was the first toy to be advertised on television. It's still a classic today.

1983

Cabbage Patch Kids were cute little dolls that also pitted parents against each other in a fight for the last one in the store.

1959

Barbie made her debut this year. Today over a billion Barbie dolls have been sold in more than 150 countries.

1989

Game Boy was Nintendo's first handheld game console. It provided hours of portable entertainment.

1995

Kids went crazy for Beanie Babies—cute big-eyed stuffed animals that fit in the palm of your hand.

1996

Tickle Me Elmo was so popular that people fought over the talking red doll in stores.

1998

Have you ever heard of Furby? This birdlike electronic robot can blink and learn English words.

1999

Anything from the Pokémon franchise is still a hit among kids and adults alike.

2000

Over five million Razor scooters were sold within the first six months of launching.

2001

A line of fashion dolls called Bratz gave Barbie a run for her money in popularity.

2007

The iPod Touch was the first iPod ever to have a touchscreen. It let people use the internet and apps.

2010

The Apple iPad was the first handheld portable tablet on the market. It was so popular that 15 million first-generation devices were sold.

2012

The Wii U had cool HD graphics and was a big hit.

2016

Nintendo's NES Classic gaming system was so popular, Nintendo had to stop making it because they couldn't keep up with demand.

2022

Wearable activity-tracking devices, smartwatches and plastic coding robots were favorites.

What is the best gift you ever got? Some people love electronics, while others like outdoor equipment. One thing is for sure—the kinds of gifts we give have changed a lot over the years.

TOYING WITH CHANGE

Around the world, change is happening. Big and small players are making it easier to give gifts that are better for the planet and kids.

NEW, NATURAL TOYS

Many toy companies are becoming more socially responsible and coming up with entire lines of toys and packaging made with environmentally friendly materials. They're switching to **bioplastics**, easy-to-recycle packaging and products that are recyclable or made with recycled materials. Some even teach kids about the planet. Here are a few highlights:

LEGO's leaves, bushes and trees are now made with bioplastic sourced from sugarcane, a sustainable raw material. The Danish company is working to use all sustainable materials in its products and packaging by 2030.

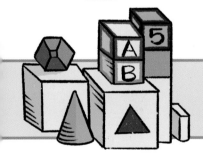

Remember those building blocks you loved when you were little? Now companies are making them from cork, a renewable wood.

Babies drool over Sophie the Giraffe. It's made from 100 percent natural rubber.

Shore Buddies is a line of toys made from recycled plastic, each one representing a marine animal endangered by ocean plastics. Another line of toys called EcoKins offers stuffed animals made from old water bottles. Each toy has a tag that tells kids how many water bottles were reused to make the stuffing, fabric and stitching.

Land of Dough makes a kind of putty that uses plant-based colors, **ethically sourced** ingredients and glitter that can be composted. The dough is made in a factory that is powered by wind and uses **reclaimed landfill gas** as a heat source.

Speaking of alternative energy, wind turbine experiment kits teach kids how to build their own wind turbine, which can then be used to power a rechargeable battery.

A new building set from France is called CLIP IT. It features magnetized recycled plastic bottle caps that can be used to create everything from buildings to art. Now some children's drinks even come with CLIP IT sets so kids can magnetize their bottle caps and use them with the rest of the set.

.SHOCK/GETTY IMAGES

A Dutch toy manufacturer has partnered with a refrigeration company to create a stacking-and-balancing game using "stones" made from recycled fridges collected from across Europe. Fight gravity and compete against friends with Rockeees.

A company from California called Green Toys has been making toy trucks, cars and boats from recycled milk jugs since 2007. This company teaches kids about the importance of recycling while also enabling them to have fun.

LIKE

BEEP, BEEP!

The green movement is accelerating. The next generation of kids is becoming greener too. A 2019 report found that 63 percent of kids your age would like to work in a field in which they can help save the planet when they grow up.

RECYCLING RAMPS UP

Two of the biggest toy companies, Hasbro and Mattel, are working with a recycling company called TerraCycle. In the United Kingdom, United States and an expanding list of countries, people can drop off or mail in Hasbro toys and games like Transformers and My Little Pony. TerraCycle melts down the plastic and turns it into things like playgrounds, benches and planters. In 2018 Hasbro began using more sustainable packaging, like plant-based plastic, and by the end of 2022 had eliminated almost all single-use plastic from new product packaging. In Canada, Mattel (which makes toys such as Barbie, Hot Wheels and American Girl) wants schools and other organizations to return their Mega Bloks toys with a prepaid shipping label. Mattel has pledged to use only recycled, recyclable or bio-based plastic materials in its toys and packaging by 2030.

Once you've outgrown playing with Barbies or Hot Wheels, you can now recycle them. That's because toy companies are getting greener.
YUPHAYAO PHANKHAMKERD/GETTY IMAGES

SHIPPING GETS SMARTER

A toy maker called Zuru has found a way to lessen its carbon footprint. Zuru's Tiny Town ride-on vehicles stack together for easy shipping and storage. Five times as many toys can fit in the same space, meaning one box can replace five!

You can make fun toys and great gifts out of things you already have at home. Use your imagination to craft a stuffed monster with multiple eyes!
ZOLOTAOSEN/GETTY IMAGES

CHOO-CHOO-CHOOSING REPAIR CAFÉS

Hans-Joachim Simon is a computer scientist in Germany. When his kids were little, he'd add to or fix their toy trains by buying parts at flea markets. He once made a train track so big that 14 trains could run on the tracks at the same time. Now he's fixing other kids' trains. His company is called Papa, mach ganz! (Fix it, Dad!). He has lots of extra parts for toy trains made by companies like LEGO and Playmobil, and he offers how-to guides so parents can fix their kids' toys at home. As long as people want their toys to last longer rather than throwing them out, he's happy to teach people how to fix them themselves.

The fix-it trend is catching on in Europe. Repair shops began popping up in the Netherlands in the late 2000s. Today there are about 2,000 repair cafés around the world.

KEEPING THINGS IN STOCK

In Germany "right to repair" laws ensure manufacturers give customers access to spare parts and repair instructions so people can fix their household appliances and extend the lives of their products. It keeps things like lamps and toasters from being thrown out when they could be fixed.

TOY LIBRARIES ARE TAKING OFF

Why buy your own toys when you can share? There are about 400 toy libraries in the United States, and many more around the world. Some charge a monthly fee to borrow toys, and others are free. It saves parents money and is better for the planet. Why? When kids get tired of playing with their toys, they can exchange them for something new. In Malaysia teachers can borrow toys for their classes, and families in apartment buildings have access to toys in common areas. Special workshops teach kids how to fix, build, upcycle, recycle and even regift.

SUSTAINABLE GIFTS FOR BIGGER KIDS

You're probably wondering what kind of gifts you can give that won't harm the planet. Here are some incredible—and incredibly sustainable—gift ideas, plus creative ways to wrap them. There's something for everyone on your list.

FOR ATHLETES

A new kind of skateboard is "wheely" cool. It's made of bamboo, a more eco-friendly, sustainable material than maple, which is what's typically used. Bamboo is a good alternative, since one in five wild maple trees are threatened by **unsustainable logging**, climate change, **deforestation** and forest fires. Even surfboards can be made more sustainably. Instead of making them from **polystyrene**, which can take 500 years to break down, some companies, like Australia's Spooked Kooks, are making them from 100 percent recycled plastic waste. They even encourage surfers to bring back the boards to be recycled when they want a new board.

Cardboard boxes can be used to make costumes for a play you put on for your friends. You can even ask an adult to help cut boxes to make things like airplanes that you can wear!

(LEFT) WUNDERVISUALS/GETTY IMAGES; (ABOVE) FLASHPOP/GETTY IMAGES

FOR CREATIVE AND CRAFTY KIDS

Sarah Turner is a UK-based eco-artist who turns discarded soda cans into art. She cleans the colorful cans, cuts them into shapes like hearts, dogs and cars, and sells them as framed pieces of art. She's also upcycled plastic bottles into bouquets of roses and made gigantic sculptures out of trash like cups, bags, bottle caps, disposable cutlery, coffee-cup lids, straws, broken tents, popped airbeds and even personal plastic face shields from the pandemic. You can get lots of ideas from her work on ways to be creative with objects you can find in your own home—or in the garbage!

FOR BEAUTY BUFFS

A Canadian chain called Green and Frugal sells eco-friendly, safe body-care products, including shampoos, body butters and deodorants, without single-use packaging. Shoppers can bring in their own glass jars and choose the products to go

LIKE

CHEW ON THIS

One day we might all be able to give greener plastic gifts. In 2016 a team of Japanese scientists discovered a kind of bacteria that can break down, or eat, **PET plastic**, the kind of plastic that soda bottles and many other things are made of. (Plastics make up about 20 percent of the volume in landfills.) The discovery has spurred researchers in other parts of the world to find more plastic-eating bacteria. In Germany, for instance, scientists are researching how to break down a kind of plastic used to make shoes.

in them. Staff fill the jars, weigh them and send home happy customers—without plastic shopping bags, naturally! You can even find recipes or kits to make beauty products yourself.

FOR GAMERS

Discarded fishing nets are responsible for 10 percent of plastic pollution in the ocean. A company called Bureo is doing its part to change this. It collects discarded nets and transforms them into a material that can be used to make everything from clothing to sunglasses to skateboards—and the building-block game called Jenga. Jenga Ocean is the first game ever to be made from recycled fishing nets. The game also teaches players about how fishing nets and other plastics are hurting ocean life and how people can help. Each game prevents over 2.2 pounds (1 kilogram) of discarded net from

Some companies are using plastic and netting pulled from the oceans to create games and toys.
(MAIN) PLACEBO365/GETTY IMAGES;
(INSET) CAVAN IMAGES/GETTY IMAGES

THE SMELL OF SUCCESS

Hart Main was just 13 years old when he had a bright idea for a way to earn some extra money to buy himself a bike. His sister made scented candles, but he didn't like how they smelled. Hart thought of making candles that would appeal to boys. His parents challenged him to follow through and start a business. That's when Hart invented ManCans. They're candles with masculine scents like bacon and sawdust. He collected empty soup cans from food banks in Ohio and used them as the candle holders. "One of my favorite lessons I enjoy sharing with other kids is to not limit yourself or think you're too young to make a difference," says Hart. Today he's in his 20s and a graduate student. His business is still thriving. Now he gets recycled soup cans from manufacturers and donates a portion of the proceeds to food banks and others in need in Ohio, Michigan, Pennsylvania and West Virginia. He has sold over 120,000 candles and donated the same number of meals as part of his One Candle, One Meal movement. His company employs people with developmental difficulties and has trained more than 140 individuals.

DBA BEAVER
CREEK CANDLE
COMPANY

entering the ocean. The company, founded by Americans who work with fishing communities in Chile, partners with leading companies like Patagonia to get its material into their products. So far Bureo has collected more than 7 million pounds (3 million kilograms) of discarded fishing nets.

SUPER SAVER

That's a Rap!

When Toronto high school student Kesh Lantz wants to give a gift, she makes sure it's extra special—and extra sustainable. "Ever since I was six years old, I've loved making gifts that are thoughtful and meaningful," she says. She often starts a gift weeks in advance to be sure it's perfect. She thinks about what each person might love and need.

"Some of my favorite gifts are '100 reasons why I love you' in a jar, digital slideshows filled with pictures and videos, custom music playlists and personalized raps," says Lantz. "I spend at least two hours writing the lyrics, finding a funny costume and putting on some makeup. Then I practice the rap, film it and send it."

The best part is the reaction she gets when the recipient watches the rap. Sometimes people laugh so hard they cry. "No matter the holiday or the occasion, it makes me feel good to give from the heart," she says.

Lantz's homemade gifts are affordable and were all made with items she already had in her home. You can do the same. Other homemade gift ideas you can try include:

- SPEND TIME WITH YOUR FRIEND BY GIVING THEM AN EXPERIENCE, LIKE A TRIP TO A MUSEUM OR SPORTING EVENT.
- BAKE COOKIES OR CUPCAKES.
- MAKE TISSUE-PAPER FLOWERS.
- MAKE A PERSONALIZED COLLAGE OR PIECE OF ART.
- MAKE A DONATION TO A SPECIAL CAUSE IN THEIR NAME.
- MAKE FRIENDSHIP BRACELETS.
- GIFT YOUR FAVORITE BOOKS. WRITE A SPECIAL MESSAGE ON THE INSIDE COVER.
- MAKE POPCORN FOR AN AT-HOME MOVIE NIGHT.
- KNIT OR SEW SOMETHING—BE CREATIVE.

When someone is down you know how to make them feel better

FOR JEWELRY LOVERS

Many charities sell bracelets that help the planet and other causes too. Bead the Change, for example, sells bracelets made of 100 percent recycled glass beads. Even the bracelet cord is made out of the material used to make recycled plastic water bottles and other products, called *rPET*. A percentage of the income from each bracelet sold supports various causes, such as reforestation, ocean cleanup and the fight against climate change. Another company called 4Ocean is dedicated to cleaning oceans, rivers and coastlines. For every bracelet sold, 4Ocean pulls a pound (almost half a kilogram) of trash from the ocean. The nonprofit raises awareness of the problem of single-use plastics and also donates a portion of proceeds to other organizations that care about the oceans too.

Wrapping gifts without using paper is a more sustainable and even beautiful way to do it.
EVGENIIA SIIANKOVSKAIA/GETTY IMAGES

LIKE

WRAP IT UP

If you want your gift to be as sustainable as it can be, don't forget to wrap it wisely. Reuse gift bags and wrapping paper, or bundle it beautifully in fabric. In Japan, gifts are wrapped in fabric called *furoshiki*. (The term refers to both the cloth and the craft itself.) Traditionally these fabrics were repurposed and used like shopping bags to hold groceries or books. Using cloth for wrapping is part of the *zero-waste movement*—people are using fabric they already have at home to wrap gifts of all shapes and sizes.

Some waste-free stores encourage you to bring your own reusable containers when you shop.
MONKEY BUSINESS IMAGES/ SHUTTERSTOCK.COM

USE YOUR POWER WISELY

Buying only sustainable products is a big goal. It will take time to change our shopping patterns. But small changes to your buying habits and what you choose to buy or not buy can make a big difference. Doing simple things like keeping your phone a little longer, giving thoughtful homemade gifts, refusing single-use plastics at restaurants and thinking about clothing purchases will help people and the planet. In the process you will also inspire your friends and classmates to do the same. If everyone does their part, even a little part, we can look forward to a healthier future.

While researching this book, I decided to make changes too. I'm not going to stop buying clothes or gifts. And I'm

You can still enjoy giving and getting gifts, but remember to use your purchasing power wisely.
ASCENT/PKS MEDIA INC./GETTY IMAGES

not going to avoid plastic products altogether or keep my cell phone until 2050. But I have become more thoughtful about what I buy, how much I buy and where I buy it. If I can buy e-gift cards, I do. I bought a new reusable coffee cup that I use every day. As I write, I'm wearing pants made from recycled plastic and shoes made from algae. I'm feeling pretty cool right now because all my new purchases have the power to influence change. Yours can too. So go out and shop till you drop. Just use your wallet wisely.

LIKE

CELEBRATE *NOT* SHOPPING!

Add this to your calendar—
BUY NOTHING DAY!
Held in November every year since 1992, the day is a global protest against *consumerism* (buying too much) and our throw-away culture. People put away their credit cards for the day, collect coats for people in need or organize thrifting parties. Can you think of ways you can participate?

Glossary

biodegrades—breaks down by the action of living things

bioplastics—plastic materials made from renewable sources, such as vegetable fats and oils, cornstarch, straw and recycled food waste

bisphenol A (BPA)—a chemical used to make certain plastics, found in food containers, water bottles and other products we use every day. It can seep into food and drinks from the containers and may be harmful to our health.

carbon dioxide (CO_2)—a colorless gas released into the air when animals breathe, when animal and vegetable matter decays and when we burn fossil fuels. It's known as a greenhouse gas because it traps heat. Too much carbon dioxide in the air causes the earth to heat up.

Certified B Corporation—a business that meets high standards of social and environmental performance, taking care of workers and the planet

child laborers—children who work for little or no money to make products for wealthier countries. Globally there are about 168 million child laborers.

climate change—the long-term changes in worldwide temperatures and weather patterns caused by human activities such as burning fossil fuels

climate emergency—a critical state in which urgent action is needed to reduce or halt climate change and its potentially irreversible environmental effects that threaten the survival of life on earth

consumerism—buying more products and services than we really need

Cradle to Cradle Certified—a global standard for products that are made safely and responsibly

deforestation—the chopping down (clearing) of forests

developing countries—countries with little economic and industrial activity and whose citizens tend to have lower incomes

ethically sourced—chosen from businesses whose products and services were obtained in ethical, responsible and sustainable ways

e-waste—discarded electrical and electronic devices, such as phones, laptops, TVs, gaming systems and tablets

fast fashion—the mass production of low-quality trendy clothes that are made quickly and cheaply and are often thrown out after only a few wearings

fossil fuels—nonrenewable fuels such as oil, coal and natural gas that are formed in the earth over millions of years from plant and animal remains

Fridays for Future—an international movement to protest the lack of action on climate change. It's made up of students

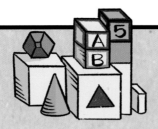

who skip classes on Friday to participate in demonstrations that push for leaders to take climate change seriously.

frugal—careful about the amount of money one spends

furoshiki—a square piece of fabric used to wrap gifts and carry items, or even in home decor. The word refers to the craft and the cloth itself.

Global Organic Textile Standard—the leading standard that assures customers that an organic fabric was made in environmentally and socially responsible ways

greenhouse gas—a gas that traps the sun's heat in the atmosphere and contributes to global warming

incinerating—burning to ashes

linear versus circular—in a linear economy raw materials are processed into a product that is thrown away after it's used. In a circular economy, raw materials are turned into a product that can be recycled into a new product at the end of its life rather than being thrown out.

living wage—the hourly wage a worker must earn to pay their basic expenses

microplastics—tiny pieces of plastic, 0.2 inches (5 millimeters) or smaller in diameter, that don't break down and which contain chemicals harmful to humans and animals

per- and polyfluoroalkyl substances (PFAS)—human-made chemicals, used on everything from food packing to stain-resistant clothing, that accumulate in and seriously harm the environment and our bodies

pesticides—chemicals sprayed on crops to kill or repel bugs so they won't eat crops

PET plastic—polyethylene terephthalate, a strong, clear plastic used for food and drink containers and fibers for clothing

phthalates—a group of chemicals used to make plastics more durable, flexible and long-lasting

polystyrene—a rigid type of plastic often used to make clear products, like food packaging or lab equipment

polyvinyl chloride (PVC)—the world's third-most-used plastic, used for pipes, doors, windows and more

reclaimed landfill gas—the gas created when garbage decomposes in a landfill and, instead of escaping into the air, is captured, converted and used as a renewable energy resource

retail therapy—shopping to improve your mood or feel better

rPET—recycled polyethylene terephthalate (PET)

semivolatile organic compounds—chemicals that evaporate into the air from a solid or liquid form, found in many plastic products

single-use plastics—items that are meant to be used only once, like a straw or plastic fork

sustainable—able to meet the needs of people and the environment now and in the future. Using resources in a sustainable way means not fully depleting them or damaging the natural world

sustainable gifts—gifts that have a smaller carbon footprint because they are made rather than bought or are bought with the health of the planet in mind

sweatshops—shops or factories in which people work long hours for low wages, usually in unhealthy working conditions

"ugly" vegetables—vegetables that are misshapen or not the typical size and don't meet supermarket standards. They are still good to eat but often get thrown away. Ugly fruit suffers the same fate.

United Nations—an organization of 193 countries whose goal is to maintain international peace and security

unsustainable logging—the practice of cutting down trees without thinking about the environment or the animals who rely on those forests

World Health Organization (WHO)—an agency of the United Nations responsible for international public health

zero-waste movement—an organized effort to promote a lifestyle that produces little or no garbage

Resources

PRINT

Barr, Catherine, and Steve Williams.
*The Story of Climate Change: A
First Book about How We Can
Help Save Our Planet*. Frances
Lincoln Children's Books, 2021.

Bell, Lucy. *You Can Change the World:
The Kids' Guide to a Better Planet*.
Andrews McMeel Publishing, 2020.

Clinton, Chelsea. *Start Now!
You Can Make a Difference*.
Philomel Books, 2018.

Harman, Alice. *Climate Change
and How We'll Fix It*. Sterling
Children's Books, 2020.

Kirby, Loll. *Old Enough to Save the Planet*.
Magic Cat Publishing, 2020.

Klein, Naomi, and Rebecca Stefoff.
*How to Change Everything:
The Young Human's Guide to
Protecting the Planet and Each
Other*. Puffin Canada, 2022.

Lerwill, Ben. *Climate Rebels*.
Puffin Books, 2020.

Mulder, Michelle. *Pocket Change:
Pitching In for a Better World*.
Orca Book Publishers, 2016.

Mulder, Michelle. *Trash Talk: Moving
Toward a Zero-Waste World*.
Orca Book Publishers, 2021.

Veness, Kimberley. *Let's Eat: Sustainable
Food for a Hungry Planet*. Orca
Book Publishers, 2017.

WEBSITES

Adria Vasil: adriavasil.com

Beaver Creek Candle Company:
bccandle.com

Earth Saver Girl: earthsavergirl.com

EcoSchools Canada: ecoschools.ca

Fashion Revolution:
fashionrevolution.org

Freecycle: freecycle.org

Good On You: goodonyou.eco

Greenpeace: greenpeace.org

Habitat for Humanity: habitat.org

iFixit: ifixit.com

iPadRehab: iPadRehab.com

Kids Against Palm Oil:
kidsagainstpalmoil.org

NASA Climate Kids: climatekids.nasa.gov

Plant for the Planet: plant-for-the-planet.org

Repair Café: repaircafe.org/en

Streetbank: streetbank.com

Suppli: mysuppli.ca

Threading Change: threadingchange.org

Tru Earth: tru.earth

University of California Climate Lab: universityofcalifornia.edu/climate-lab

Young Reporters for the Environment: yre.global

DOCUMENTARIES AND VIDEOS

"Curb Your Carbon." *The Nature of Things*, season 61, episode 6, 2022. cbc.ca

GPS: Garbology. PBS: pbslearningmedia.org

The Plastic Problem. PBS NewsHour documentary, 2019. youtube.com/watch?v=1RDc2opwg0I

Recycled Threads. PBS: pbslearningmedia.org

Rethinking Fast Fashion After Bangladesh. Audio essay. PBS: pbslearningmedia.org

A Sustainable Seafood Restaurant | NOAA Fisheries. PBS: pbslearningmedia.org

Toxic Clothing. CBC: cbc.ca

The True Cost of Fast Fashion | EcoSense for Living. PBS: pbslearningmedia.org

"'We would slash the fabric': Fashion's Harmful Habit of Destroying Unsold Clothes." Global News: globalnews.ca

Acknowledgments

Writing a book with four separate topics was like writing several books at once. I relied on so many people for help with each chapter. Thank you to Adria Vasil, author of the Ecoholic book series, for her vast expertise and experience in the eco-warrior sphere and for her generosity in suggesting other experts to interview. Adria helped me find a range of amazing programs, initiatives and experts for each topic, including Sophia Yang of Threading Change, Julianna Greco from Suppli and the amazing zero-waste consultant and speaker Sophi Robertson of Your Eco Friend. From there, I found EcoSchools and Young Reporters for the Environment, plus the unstoppable Sophia Mathur. I was thrilled to discuss e-waste with iFixit's Elizabeth Chamberlain. I also had a great discussion with Dr. Jessa Jones, who gave me some really helpful tips on how kids can extend the life of their devices. I had no idea dry rice won't fix my phone if I've dropped it in water! I spoke with the thoughtful, delightful and energetic Kesh Lantz, who makes amazing homemade gifts and whose gifting ideas will inspire other teens. I've been the recipient of one of her personalized rap videos myself—it's truly the zero-waste gift that keeps on giving. I also want to give a big thanks to the team at Orca for believing in my ideas and giving me the chance to research and write books that I know will make a difference to readers and the planet. I am so happy and fulfilled getting to do what I love while also being a positive force for change.

Index

PAGE NUMBERS IN **BOLD** INDICATE AN IMAGE CAPTION.

Erin Silver is an award-winning children's author. Her books include *Just Watch Me* (Krystal Kite Award nominee), *What Kids Did: Stories of Kindness and Invention in the Time of COVID-19* (Hackmatack Award nominee), *Proud to Play: LGBTQ+ Athletes Who Made History, Rush Hour: Navigating Our Global Traffic Jam* (Blueberry Award winner), *Sitting Shiva* (Vine Award finalist, TD Canadian Children's Literature Award finalist) and *Good Food, Bad Waste: Let's Eat for the Planet* (2024 American Association for the Advancement of Science/Subaru SB&F Prize for Excellence in Science Books finalist). Erin was chosen to tour during Canadian Children's Book Week in 2023 and is a sought-after speaker at schools, libraries and conferences. She has an MFA in creative nonfiction and a postgraduate journalism degree. Erin lives in Toronto.

Suharu Ogawa is a Toronto-based illustrator. Her love for drawing started in a kindergarten art school after being kicked out of calligraphy class for refusing to convert to right-handedness. Formally trained in art history and cultural anthropology, she worked for several years as a university librarian until her passion for illustration called her out of that career and into the pursuit of a lifelong dream. Since then, Suharu has created illustrations for magazines, public art projects and children's books, including *Why Humans Work: How Jobs Shape Our Lives and Our World* in the Orca Think series. She also teaches illustration at OCAD University in Toronto.

THE MORE YOU KNOW
THE MORE YOU GROW

TAKING CARE OF WHERE WE LIVE

Ecosystems

MERRIE-ELLEN WILCOX

LET'S GET CREATIVE

ART FOR A HEALTHY PLANET

JESSICA ROSE ILLUSTRATED BY JARETT SITTER

ALSO BY ERIN SILVER

IN IT TO WIN IT

SPORTS AND THE CLIMATE CRISIS

ERIN SILVER

ILLUSTRATED BY PUI YAN FONG

ALONE TOGETHER

A CURIOUS EXPLORATION OF LONELINESS

PETTI FONG

ILLUSTRATED BY JONATHAN DYCK

REMEMBER THIS

The Fascinating World of Memory

Monique Polak

Illustrated by Valéry Goulet

ALSO BY ERIN SILVER

GOOD FOOD, BAD WASTE

Let's Eat for the Planet

Erin Silver

Illustrated by Suharu Ogawa

OPEN SCIENCE

KNOWLEDGE FOR EVERYONE

MONIQUE POLAK

ILLUSTRATED BY CATHERINE CHAN

BREAKING NEWS

WHY MEDIA MATTERS

RAINA DELISLE

Illustrated by Julie McLaughlin

SAVE NATURAL HABITATS!!

RIGHT TO LIVE

RIGHT to SPEAK UP!

EQUALITY = FOR = ALL

Right to Live Free of Discrimination

WHAT'S THE BIG IDEA?

The **Orca Think** series introduces us to the issues making headlines in the world today. It encourages us to question, connect and take action for a better future. With those tools we can all become better citizens. Now that's smart thinking!

RIGHT TO LEARN